SAM'S PLACE
STORIES

By
Bob Mustin

www.AuthorMikeInk.com

ISBN: 978-0-9852146-6-1
Library of Congress Control Number: 2013931764

First Published by *AuthorMike Ink*, 3/25/2013

www.AuthorMikeInk.com

AuthorMike Ink and its logo are trademarked by *AuthorMike Ink Publishing*.

Printed in the United States of America

TABLE OF CONTENTS

A LONG RUN OF LUCK

The scarlet and white neon sign hanging over the entry to Sam's Place began to swing, adding its creaks to the cold front's moan. As the sign swayed, crimson shadows swept to and fro over scalloped gravel in the pool hall's parking lot. A rangy teen-aged boy slipped from the surrounding thicket of Alabama pine and into view, his tee shirt bleached to a luminous white by the lights of an approaching semi on the two-lane. He hurried past crumpled plastic beer cups aglow with the oncoming glare, his black, high-top canvas shoes skirting a thick, odorous pudding of puke. With little more than a glance, he passed a man and woman grinding out their lubricious urges against a pickup cab. Then he leaped and cleared the three tiers of cinderblock steps to the pool hall's threshold and opened the door to a wedge of dim light.

Inside the long, one-room building sat eight felt-covered tables, a wide aisle separating the two rows of four. An oak bar at the opposite end filled most of the building's width, a rear door to the left. Multicolored neon beer lights clung to the rear wall, bubbling and flashing, indifferent to all else. Fluorescent fixtures hung over the tables, suspended as if by some nocturnal alchemy, the light fixing ghostly images within layers of cigarette smoke.

A lanky man, shirttail out, leaned on his pool cue at the nearest table. Opposite him stood a short, bald man named Wilson, his dress shirt stained yellow at the armpits, its buttons straining to contain a drooping gut. A woman named Noxanne, her sweatshirt pushing *I ♥ BAMA* at the world, muttered irritably and glanced to Wilson. She cocked an ample hip, plumbed a pocket, and handed a gobbet of greenbacks to the lanky one. Along the plank wall adjacent to the front door, hangers-on watched, solemn as cigar store Indians, their smokes hanging from lips and fingers. The lanky man took Noxanne's money, put up his cue, slipped past the boy who had just entered, and left.

Across the aisle, a tall, stoop-shouldered man in thinning suit pants and a dress shirt with rolled-up sleeves scratched at his oily shock of graying hair, grinned, and approached his table.

"Two left," he said. "Anybody want me to call 'em?"

"No point to it, Slim," said someone along the wall. "You got too much mojo tonight." Laughter slithered through smoke and darkness.

Slim looked to his opponent, who refused to retreat from the table. Slim jabbed his cue at two corner pockets and then slid his cigarette to the table's edge. The cue ball clicked against one striped ball, then the other. The balls rumbled into their appointed pockets, and the cue ball rebounded away.

Slim's opponent slammed a boot heel into the floor planking. Without a word, he broke down his cue, pulled on his coat, and departed.

"Shitfire," someone whispered, voice tinged with awe, "you see that?"

Donnie, a short, snaggletoothed man of early middle age, offered to buy Slim a whiskey. Slim covered a cough and shook no, planted his cigarette in the thin line of his mouth, and grabbed a spray of twenties from the table's edge. He peered into the shadows. "Anybody else got a game for me?"

"No fools here," somebody said. Those around the spectator laughed – a staccato chorus of nervous praise.

Slim offered a wry smile. "Always some fool hoping to push you off the heap, though." He dragged a Coke crate from against the nearby wall, stood it on end. Setting a foot on it, he leaned an elbow onto the up-bent knee and looked from face to face. "I ever tell y'all about that time in upper state New York? I was shooting with this fellow from Ohio, see? He come up to me, drunk as all get-out, bragging and waving money, so I said 'what the hell?' Drunk as he was, he run the table on me nine straight times. Nine, I'm telling you!"

He spoke of finally beating the man, then of meeting him again in Minnesota, of playing him in the finals of a big tourney. Pausing, he licked spume from a corner of his mouth and spat a wad of dark phlegm to the plank floor.

"Did you whup 'em in Duluth, Slim?" a beery voice asked.

"Damn right. I took him for his whole stake. But I'll tell you what. If I ever see him again, I'll just shake

3

hands and ease out the door. I hear Lady Luck has been smiling real pretty for him lately."

"Ah, you'd take him, Slim."

"Maybe." Slim laughed. "Well, hell, yeah, I'd probably do just that."

The boy edged close. He reached deep and tossed a wadded bill onto Slim's table.

Sam's Place fell silent. All eyes turned.

The boy hitched at his frayed jeans. "I been watching you the past two nights, mister. You been making some fine shots, sure 'nough, but you know what? I think all that's left of you wouldn't amount to a cup of spit. The reason you like playing folks in Mister Sam's place is 'cause you're washed-up. A has-been." He stood, legs apart, and combed a sweep of fine, blond hair off his eyes with a bony hand.

Sam glowered from the building's rear. "Get the hell on home, Tommy."

The boy didn't move.

Sam palmed his way around the bar and lumbered toward him. "You want me to tell your mama you been in here this time of night? Go on. Git!"

The boy shifted his weight but didn't budge.

Slim chuckled. He stepped aside and headed for the bar as Sam lunged at the boy. Sam twisted Tommy's shirt collar in one ham-sized hand, jerked him to his toes, and shoved him toward the door. Whispers hissed along the wall. The bubble lights behind the bar chortled softly.

Slim drew a cup of draft from Sam's tap. Then he turned, no vestige of amusement on his face. "Don't run him off, Sam, not just yet, anyways. Send the little peckerwood down here."

Sam eyed Slim, a faint smile flickering. He shoved the boy toward the old hustler.

Tommy grinned proudly. He shrugged his shirt back into place and strode the remainder of the room's length.

"So you're a shooter, huh, kid?" said Slim.

The boy nodded.

Slim looked past, eyes dark and narrow. "What about it, boys? He any good?"

"He ain't bad," said Wilson.

Others murmured agreement.

"Who in here can beat 'me?"

Sam returned to the bar and waved a finger in the snaggletoothed man's direction. "Donnie beat him regular up until a couple months ago. Still beats him some."

Slim dipped a finger in his beer's foam, stirred, then licked the digit. He rattled out an unctuous cough. "You got any money, kid?"

"I got that ten."

"That all?"

"Yeah."

Slim shook out a cigarette from his shirt pack, lit the smoke, and leaned against the bar. "You got a big yap, boy. You ought to have money if you gonna mouth off that way." He exhaled a thread of smoke upward. "Tell you what. You find a hundred dollars, and we'll just see who whups who."

The place went graveyard quiet. The boy sighed, turned back, and pocketed the crumpled ten.

The cash register bell rang. Sam held up a fan of bills and spread them on the bar. "I'm a fool to do it, but his ten and my ninety says he gets his shot."

Slim finished his beer amid a chorus of titters. One corner of his mouth cocked upward. He neared the boy and hung an arm across his shoulders. "You got money now, kid, so let's play some ten ball. Ten racks okay with you?"

The boy swallowed and nodded.

They lagged for break. The boy won. He finished the first rack with slow, deliberate shots. After the second break, his rhythm picked up, and he made some tough shots look easy. But on his fifth rack, he left a table full of garbage. Shooting carefully, he began to clear the table. He called the four ball in a corner pocket, an open shot. His cue ball nudged the four into a slow, rumbling roll. It dropped, and the cue ball followed with a thud.

Slim approached the table without a word and finished the break. He broke again, playing quickly. Forty more balls went. Then, after three solid shots on the next rack, he missed a long one. The cue ball rattled its way to the table's far rail.

Slim sniffed to disguise an impending smirk. "Lucky break for you, huh, kid?"

The boy stared at the table. He didn't move. Then he licked his lips. Slim retreated to the bar and gathered in Sam's ninety dollars. With a card dealer's flourish, he spread the bills onto the table's edge.

Tommy eyed the bills. A drop of sweat skidded down one eyebrow. Exhaling, he mumbled, "Seven in the side." The cue ball wobbled away. It nudged the seven past the side pocket to a point a foot or so up the rail.

Slim smiled broadly for the first time since the match started. He moved to the table and picked off the remaining balls with sure, precise strokes. Rolling his stick onto the table's edge, he lit another smoke and pocketed the ninety dollars.

"That's it, sonny boy," he said.

Tommy looked about, face long, cheeks hollow. His head drooped as he turned toward the door.

"Hey, hold it," said Slim.

He turned.

"The game was a hundred dollars. I only got ninety."

The boy mumbled, pulled the crumpled ten from his pocket, and flung it to the floor.

Sam's front door slammed behind the boy.

Slim coughed again, a deep, tubercular-sounding one.

"He won't be back for a while," someone cackled.

"He ain't nothing but a boy," said Noxanne. "A little snot-nosed boy."

Slim grunted. "Kids got no damn business in pool halls." He flicked a finger at the bloody leakage at one corner of his mouth, then picked up the ten and pocketed it. He walked the other ninety back to Sam.

Donnie offered a whiskey again, and this time Slim took it. He drank it in one upturned motion and let out a long sigh.

"You sure showed him, Slim," said Wilson.

"Huh," said Slim.

"Pretty cold," said Sam. "I know we done that hustle a hundred times before, but you shouldn't rub a boy's nose in it like that."

"Goddamn it," Slim said, "he could of beat me, you hear? That boy could of beat me!"

"You didn't need to take his money," Sam said softly.

Slim huffed. "Wish somebody had run me out of pool halls when I was his age." He shivered, then snapped his fingers and pointed. Someone handed him his suit coat. He tugged it on. For a moment, he studied the floor planks at his boot toes. Then he looked up, his eyes' sheen filled with a sadness deep as the night. "I've had myself a long run of luck, a good one by anybody's account. But that boy might be right. Could be I'm played out."

"I don't expect you're goners just yet," said Sam, his words soft, almost tender.

"Yeah, Slim," came a voice from the shadows. "You still the best I ever seen."

CHAPTER I

Sunday morning had crept in on a throaty wind, softened only by a pure but raggedly applied coating of snow. Sam had risen early, fed his dog Luther, and driven two miles on the all but abandoned two-lane to his pool hall. He wouldn't open his establishment to business on a Sunday: the citizens of Striven, Alabama, its city fathers and religious leaders, wouldn't have abided it. He lit the gas space heater at one end of the bar, listened to its hollow voice for a moment, and then warmed before reading the Sunday paper.

The door opened to Donnie Wimple. Without a word, Donnie chose a house cue, racked the balls on the table nearest the heater and began shooting. Sam turned to watch. After a while, he chose a stick for himself and began a game of rotation with Donnie.

Sam's plump fingers ached with the cold still hovering in his building, the aching aggravated by arthritis and scar tissue from a long-ago Viet Cong grenade. As he attempted to line his first shot, he blinked. He adjusted his glasses. Blinking again, he swore and adjusted the glasses once more. Then he decided to turn on more lights in the ever-dim pool hall. He bent to the table. His cue ball chased after its object. Both dropped into a corner pocket.

Donnie shot and missed, and then he watched without his usual brash comments as Sam lined another shot. The ball failed to drop at a mid-table pocket, and the cue ball clumped its way back up the rail, leaving Donnie a perfect shot at the far corner. Donnie

9

smirked now, and was about to offer a jibe. Before he could speak, Sam slammed his cue to the table and stalked away.

THE FAITHFUL CITY

The door to Sam's Place creaked open to an oppressive wedge of summer afternoon heat. An aged stick of a man bent and entered. He doffed his fedora – the broad-brimmed kind worn to keep the sun's malevolence from an already parched neck and face. At the first table, scrawny shooter Donnie eyed the man and spun twin streams of cigarette smoke from his crooked nose.

"Hey, dum-dum," he called out, "close the damn door."

The older man stepped aside to allow a young, gaunt woman to enter. Then, with a hard look, he strode to Donnie's table. "You, sir," he said in his resonant preacher's voice, "are a heathen cur." He grabbed Donnie's neck with one talon-like hand and squeezed.

Donnie's face bulged red. The cigarette he'd wedged into a gap between his snaggled teeth fell to the floor, issuing a cascade of tiny embers.

Sam woke from his doze at the building's rear and fumbled his way around the oaken bar. Shoes scuffled to make way for him.

The spindly woman stood to the preacher's side, hands together at her breast, as if a dog begging scraps. "Papa," she said, "you have to let 'em go. It hardly serves the Lord's purposes to hurt 'em now."

11

Before Sam could force his round frame into the mildly odorous encounter, the old man let Donnie go.

Donnie squawked, then bent to retrieve his smoke. He eyed the old man. "I know you now, you old sumbitch, you're that wandering preacher."

The old man sniffed. He canted into a barely noticeable bow. "Leviticus Withers, God's servant." One arm swept in a graceful arc before his daughter. "And Dorene, one of His own angels." He regarded Donnie with a long squint. "And who might you be? I wish to remember those who malign the Lord."

"I ain't m'ligned nothing," Donnie mumbled. He crawfished back a step and rubbed his throat's blush.

Sam now stood behind Donnie. He set his hands on the shooter's bony shoulders. "Hang your hat and stay a while, Leviticus," he said to the preacher. "What brings you back to good ol' Alabam'?"

The preacher pressed his thin lips into a smile and handed his hat to Dorene, who scurried away to a wall peg. He brushed at his shiny gabardine coat with the back of one hand, as if to remove something of Donnie from it. "The Lord's will brought me back to this den of iniquity," he said, "to save lost souls." He drew a stack of bi-folded brochures from an inside coat pocket and turned to Dorene. "Daughter, give each of these sinners a bit of testimony, if you please."

She took the religious broadsides and scuttled about the hall proffering them to Sam's flock.

"You come back, huh?" said Noxanne. "You gonna mess up our afternoon's sport, ain't you?" She slid the butt end of her cue to the floor, as if it were a lance. She stood, thick legs apart, cutoff jeans flared upward from her crotch like wings aloft. The too-small tee shirt stretched over her generous breasts warned: MAKE YOUR MOVE.

"Papa," Dorene whispered in overloud fashion, "didn't we bring her to the Lord last time we passed through?"

The preacher took in Noxanne, from gold lamé sandals to her frizzy mane. "I remember, daughter," he said, "but she's surely backslid and once more a magnet for whoremongers."

"You old buzzard," said Noxanne. "I thought when we had our moment last time you passed through that you was right with the Lord. But since then I been getting the goods on you. Now I got a mind to whomp you for being such a –" She paused, trying to divine the right word. "– philanderer."

Leviticus' face flushed. He grabbed for her cue.

She jerked it out of reach and began to spar with the old man's flailing arm.

Sam yanked the cue from her. "All right!" he said. "You two gonna have at each other, go outside. I got customers peaceably passing time."

Noxanne eyed the preacher and said, "Don't *no*body get to judge *me*."

Sam hung a beefy arm across the preacher's slight shoulders and led him to the bar, where neon beer lights on the rear wall continued their bubbling. The preacher leaned his elbows on the bar's oaken top and hiked a boot

13

onto the brass foot rail. He sighed. Sam dropped two shot glasses between them, and poured a dollop of whiskey into each. The preacher took in half his drink, and Sam poured more.

"You look like you ain't been eating regular," said Sam. "Hard times?"

Leviticus ran a finger around the rim of his glass. "Not much call these days for a preacher who ain't been educated at seminary."

Meanwhile, Dorene had found a home for each of the brochures. Donnie blinked as he bent to his copy. He silently mouthed the words his fingertip underlined. "What's this here mean? 'How is the faithful city becoming a harlot? It was full of judgment; righteousness lodged in it; but now murderers.' You saying somebody in here murdered somebody?"

Dorene stood primly before Donnie. "They quit judging," she said. "It's the reason Nineveh and all them other cities fell."

Sam sipped from his glass. "You come in awful edgy, Leviticus. I guess Noxanne hit you in a sore spot."

The preacher gave a shrug that implied maybe. He looked away.

Sam studied him for a long minute. "I'm still thinking you ain't cut out for saving souls."

The preacher glanced up. "It's true, I did give the laboring side of life a try more'n once, thanks to you, but I ain't found nothing there but hardship. There ain't nothing left for me but the Lord's work."

Sam's unkempt eyebrows drew together over his broad nose as he considered this. "You're still a mighty fine speaker, Leviticus. Ever think about organizing? They's a crowd over at the paper mill talking about a union."

Leviticus sniffed his whiskey, peered into its brown depths.

"That don't make a whole lot of sense," Donnie said to Dorene. "I thought we wasn't s'posed to make judgments."

Dorene squirmed. She glanced to the bar, but her father was to be of no help. "It's the judgments that keeps ever'body faithful," she said.

Donnie sent a soft, staccato whistle through the gap in his teeth. "Lessee. If I read you right, then, this faithful city is bad 'cause its people took up some bad ways, and nobody's passing judgment?"

Dorene nodded. "The Good Book says make straight the way of the Lord. That's what the judgment does, it keeps ever'body on the straight and narrow."

A throng began to gather.

Sam craned forward, ear cocked to the crowd's rising hum. "Looks like Donnie and Dorene's got a good one going."

"The Good Lord won't allow me no leeway," said Leviticus. His head dropped so low he seemed to be talking to his glass.

"Those folks at the mill," said Sam, "they got their hearts in the right place. They just need somebody to put

15

words to their sit'ation. They don't aim to ask for much, just some health insurance, and other such items."

Noxanne elbowed her way into the gathering's inner circle. "Judge not, that ye be not judged," she said. "For with what judgment ye judge, ye shall be judged; and with what measure ye mete, it shall be measured to you again." She nodded.

The crowd, including Donnie and Dorene, turned to her.

"What the hell," said Archie, a tall, hunch-shouldered man.

"She's right, no doubt about that," said Wilson, Noxanne's newly fledged paramour. He hooked an arm about her plump waist. "You gotta be careful what you say, 'cause what goes around comes around."

"I learnt that verse word for word," said Noxanne, as she turned a glare on Dorene, "'fore I got the goods on your randy old rascal of a daddy. So don't you judge me."

The crowd hushed. A horsefly wove graceful patterns over them before settling on Wilson's bald head. He swatted. The fly spiraled into the cobwebbed rafters.

"Seems, though," said Sam, "that you been taking this calling of yours too much to heart."

Leviticus drained his glass. Sam refilled it. Leviticus' eyes flicked toward Noxanne, and he began rubbing his forehead. "I'm bound by my sins," he said in one long, sad breath. "I have to repent. I have to take my meals from locusts and honey."

Dorene's eyelids began to twitch. She tried to blink the tic away. "Well, somebody's got to judge. That's how it's been revealed to Papa and me as the Lord's own servants. We got to act as His instruments."

Wilson pulled Noxanne closer. He smiled, widening his double chin. In a loud voice, he said to Dorene, "Shoot, girl, it'll all come out in the wash."

Sam smiled wryly at Wilson's pronouncement. "Leviticus," he said, "I can't think of anything you done in all the years I known you that'd call for eating grasshoppers. Don't think like that, it'll drive you crazy."

"I've sinned," Leviticus mumbled into his whiskey. "I've sinned terribly."

Dorene bounced on the balls of her feet and waved her hands in tiny circles. "It don't come out in no wash," she said. She tapped a skeletal forefinger on Wilson's stomach bulge. "Except if you repent and accept Jesus' saving hand."

Wilson's smile slipped away. "You trying to say it's me that's been doing the sinning 'round here? Hey, I got nothing to repent for." He huffed. "Repent my backside."

Noxanne chortled. "Ass," she said. "That's what he meant. His backside is his ass." She glanced at Wilson's rear. "And a fine one it is."

Wilson's eyes flitted across the floor and its quilt of dust and boot leavings before returning to Dorene. "Noxanne don't mean to cause upset, ma'am. She just can't help but say things like that."

"That's all right," said Dorene, her gaze lifted to the rafters and the metal roof's corrugated underside. "I expect to hear the worst in a place like this."

Leviticus motioned for Sam to lean closer. Sam did.

"The worst of it concerns my daughter," said Leviticus.

The air conditioning unit behind Sam had dropped into another gear, and its air slipped a notch in temperature. He rubbed at the gooseflesh on his arms. "Dorene? I'm real sorry. I heard about her mama dying, and all –"

"That's just it," said Leviticus. "She didn't."

Donnie took a step toward Dorene. "A place like this? What d'you mean? This is a gaming place. It ain't no worse than church league softball."

Noxanne nodded, snorting contempt.

"It's the devil's workshop," said Dorene.

"Wilma," said Leviticus, "she took Dorene in. Both of us, I guess you could say. A couple of wayfarers, straight from sin."

"We been through all this before," said Donnie. "This here's a place of recreation. A place where we can let it all hang out."

Noxanne laughed. "That oughta put a nasty picture in her mind."

"I didn't know," said Sam.

"Dorene wasn't born the angel she is now," said Leviticus.

"That's what I mean," said Dorene. "Idle hands and wicked minds, they straight out of the devil's workshop."

"Bull," said Noxanne. "That's a big old bucket of bull –" She stopped. "Bullhockey."

"I guess I don't understand," said Sam.

"A tryst," said Leviticus. "Dorene was born of a tryst."

"Profanity is blasphemy," said Dorene as she shook a finger in Noxanne's face. Her voice rose in a quivering, soprano imitation of her father's. "It shall not be forgiven."

"I didn't say no profanity," said Noxanne.

"You did," said Dorene. "Bullhockey is profanity."

"A tryst?" said Sam.

Leviticus sniffed. "Back then, I was still young in the ways of the Lord. One night, I visited a place of carnal abomination, thinking the power of the Lord was strong in me." He shook his head, ever so sadly. "Like I said, I was still a child in Him."

Noxanne elbowed Wilson away, pushed chubby fists into her hips. "I tole you, you little scamp, nobody gets to judge me!"

"Whore!" Dorene countered. She rushed at Noxanne with ragged fingernails.

The crowd surged closer.

Sam straightened, peered to the front.

"Pull her dang hair!" someone called out.

Sam drew away from the preacher. Leviticus, a step on the way to being pie-eyed, clamped Sam's arm with a bony hand.

Donnie threw his bony frame between the two women. "Hey! Sam ain't gonna stand for no fighting. Keep it up, he'll close the place down, sure as summertime."

"That's the gospel truth," Wilson said. "He'll run us all off." He pulled the scratched and gasping Noxanne to him and whispered to her as he smoothed her mussed tresses.

"I allowed two harlots to lure me to a room," Leviticus muttered, voice hoarse with emotion.

Sam squinted at the crowd. The hooting began to quiet. He let the preacher tug him back.

"We defiled our bodies," said Leviticus.

"Defiled?" said Sam. "What d'you mean defiled?"

"Lord help me," said Dorene, her gaze this time somewhere beyond the cobwebbed rafters. "I've let the Wicked One's base emotions come over me." She, too, displayed scratches, her hair a cyclone. She licked at a drop of blood that had slid from nose to upper lip and said, "Forgive me, Lord."

"Uh, uh, uh," Noxanne snubbed. She wiped away a tear.

"Defiled," said Leviticus. "You know the story of Abraham and his daughters."

Sam edged away from the preacher. He poured fresh shots.

"I don't know which one is Dorene's rightful mother," said Leviticus. He shook his head, his shot glass lost in the curl of one claw-like hand. "They was sisters. They wouldn't tell me, and Dorene favors both of 'em."

"Well," said Sam. "Well. I don't know."

"I-I'm awful sorry," Dorene bawled. "No matter what you done, you my sister in the Lord. I shouldn't of dug into you like that."

Noxanne started bawling, too. She reached, pulled Dorene to her bosom, and the two sisters in the Lord cried together.

"Good to get that one off your chest, I reckon," Sam said to Leviticus.

The preacher gave Sam a strained, embarrassed look. "Didn't mean to go on like that," he mumbled. He pulled a tarnished railroad watch from his vest pocket and unsnapped its cover. "It's almost suppertime, so I expect me and Dorene ought to go. I think we got enough for a meal and a room."

"Them folks," Sam said, lifting his chin toward the tables, "they a little rough around the edges, but they good people. If I was you, I'd pass the hat."

The preacher threw back the rest of his whiskey, straightened, and turned.

"Go on," said Sam. "You'll see."

Leviticus nodded. "Daughter, pass the hat, if you please."

Dorene ducked through the crowd, inverted her father's wide-brimmed fedora, and pushed a hollow into its blocking.

"Ladies and gentlemen," Leviticus said, "bless the Lord's work. Be generous as His angel passes among you. For this brief moment, you'll be living in the comfort of God's grace."

Dorene circled the sweaty, unmoving crowd like a border collie set to corral sheep.

No one moved. A low, snide chuckle came from the throng, then another.

"These two, they on hard times," Sam said. "Do what you can for 'em."

For another moment, nothing. Then hands began crawling into pockets. Change rattled into the hat, followed by a weak issue of folding money.

Leviticus turned to Sam. "I wouldn't'a believed them heathens –"

"They ain't that," Sam said. "They good folk." He slid two fives from his own wallet across the bar.

Leviticus plunged Sam's money into a coat pocket.

"I guess you ain't interested in that mill job, then," said Sam.

Leviticus shook his head. "Not so long as the Lord continues to bless us like this."

"That job won't be around forever," said Sam. "Handouts won't, neither."

Leviticus smiled, his eyes shining with the bliss of whiskey and unsolicited grace. He clamped Sam's hand, pumped it, and then trod to Dorene's side. He plunged fingers into the extended hat and tumbled the change and bills into a front pants pocket. "You done good, daughter," he said.

Dorene smiled and hugged the old man's arm.

The preacher reached into his coat pocket and handed the two fives to her. Dorene stuffed them into the vestal space between her slight breasts.

After carefully restoring his fedora's blocking, Leviticus gave Sam's patrons a stiff bow. He pulled Dorene to him and they passed through the door as one, disappearing into the day's final, rapturous blaze of glory.

CHAPTER II

Donnie started after Sam, but then he stopped. Sam was an even tempered fellow for the most part; moody sometimes, though, and that made him seem unpredictable and maybe even a little dangerous at times. Donnie re-racked the balls and began practicing shots.

Sam returned to his paper. Minutes passed in thick, Sunday silence. Finally, he tossed the paper in wild array to the bar and reached for the TV remote. Nothing on the broadcast channels but the usual early morning political talk shows. He flicked to ESPN. Nothing there but rehashes of the previous week's football games and a talk show emceed by two men who seemed bent on out-shouting one another.

Donnie cackled. "I s'pose we could wash up and go to meeting." Meaning church.

"In a pig's eye," Sam growled.

Donnie quietly cleared his throat. Sometimes he felt that way, too. But on other occasions, when he felt himself sinking into moral quicksand, he'd sense the flames of Hell licking at him, and for a month or so, he'd show up at the United Methodist, singing the hymns as if his heart would burst and amen-ing every other of the preacher's utterances.

"No?" he asked, altogether too timidly.

"If you had to deal with that bunch the way I have," Sam growled, "you'd think fire and brimstone was the better way to go."

"Okay," Donnie ventured, "if you say so."

24

"Go on," said Sam. *"Go on if you got a mind to. I'm staying right here in front of this fire."*

AN INTIMACY

Noxanne began to squirm. She pushed at Wilson's hairy, fish belly-white body. "Get off me, I said."

Wilson grunted, shoved his pelvis at hers one last time and rolled away, his chest hair matted. He caught his breath, turned on one side, and tried to kiss her. She pressed a palm to his face and pushed him away.

"What's the matter, sugar?"

She sniffed and placed a forearm over her eyes.

Wilson wrenched himself onto one elbow and studied her as he sang a snatch of the song they had adopted as theirs: "Lay around the shack till the mail train comes back, I'm rollin' in my sweet baby's arms."

"Shut up, Wilson. Just shut up."

He frowned. "I didn't hurt you or nothing, did I? 'Cause I know that ol' pecker of mine been known to…"

Noxanne rolled away, her back to him. He spooned into her and craned to see her face. Those features seemed to have grown puffy, as if she'd been crying for hours. Her thick bottom lip stuck out, the centerpiece of a pout.

"C'mon, babycakes, tell ol' Wilson what's going on." He brushed lightly at her frizzy red hair. She had just turned thirty-five, and a streak or two of gray were already peeking out from among those sunburst frizzes.

She reached a hand and patted his. "It ain't nothing, I guess. It's just me."

He chuckled, gave her hand a squeeze, and continued brushing at her hair.

She rolled onto her back, absently rubbing her abdomen. She squinted at him, as if trying to see through the human veneer to something certain to be lurking underneath. Then she sniffed and rubbed a tear away with one knuckle. "Oh, Wilson," she said, stifling a sob, "I'm such a tramp."

Their affair had begun as a pool shooting partnership at Sam's Place, on the outskirts of the Alabama town of Striven. It's a small town and, entertainment-wise, unadorned. It had never even had a movie theater. Its only hangout, other than Sam's Place, was the Wal-Mart parking lot, but high school kids, some two decades younger than Wilson and Noxanne had appropriated that grand spread of asphalt as their own. So Noxanne and Wilson had taken – separately – to shooting pool at Sam's, and that had led to their team-up. Neither was a shooter of renown, but together they managed to rake a healthy bit of change into their pockets playing paper mill workers who had had a gulp of beer too many.

Wilson, who had separated from his wife Lurleen some months earlier, had been the one to suggest teaming up; in fact, he'd had his eye on Noxanne as a possible paramour for quite a while, and he saw this team-up as a doorway into her good graces. Noxanne, who managed to wriggle her generous body into halter-tops and cut-off jeans in summer, or velour pedal pushers and sweatshirts in winter, and whose frizzy hair and gold lamé sandals bookended the assets Sam's customers constantly admired, seemed to Wilson the catch of the town. He was drawn to women like Noxanne: she wasn't particularly pretty, but she was brassy and free-spirited – probably compensations for having been born into the midst of four brothers – and those traits made the perfect complement to Wilson's homespun wiliness.

Besides, the other male hangers-out at Sam's proved to be the palest of competition. Most were shy, no doubt having had their personalities pummeled into dust at an early age by one parent or another, or a teacher, or a Sunday School instructor. The sort of men who were conditioned to think of Noxanne Simpwell as trashy, but who habitually closed their eyes in the shower and massaged their boners as they fantasized about her. And so this worship-from-afar made it easy for Corwin W. Noonsocket, the bald, overweight, pasty-fleshed rake known by his middle name, Wilson, to work his way into Noxanne's good graces.

He now kissed her ear. "No you ain't," he whispered. "You ain't even close to being a tramp. If you was, I wouldn't be here making sweet music with you."

Bleary-eyed, she glanced at him and blinked, as if unsure whether the words she'd just heard and the face she was seeing would align. She sniffed and looked away. Then she nudged herself a hair closer.

"That's my girl," he whispered, coaxing. He slid a hand toward her privates.

She stopped his hand's advance. "Don't, now. We

done had our playtime."

He kissed her ear again. "It ain't that easy, sugar. It's tough keeping my hands off you."

Laughing softly, she patted the hand. "I can tell that much, Wilson Noonsocket. You're just a randy ol' whore chaser, ain't you?"

He feigned shock as he edged the hand up her leg. "A whore chaser? Whatever made you think such a thing? I just like the sight of a nice leg, that's all. And a cute teardrop-shaped fanny. I see them things and, well, next thing I know I'm in bed getting a better view."

She blushed and elbowed him softly. "You need a pair of glasses, that's what you need. Otherwise, you'd see these chubby legs of mine, and my tummy that pooches out like I was with child."

His hand found the intersection of her legs. He fingered through the tuft of hair there. "You ain't like that," he said. "Leastways, that ain't how I see you."

A giggle. "Go on now. If I didn't know better, I'd think you was in love." Another glance his way, penetrating.

He edged the sheet down, baring one of her breasts. "Could be," he said as he kissed the breast. "Could be."

She nudged closer. "Why, you're stiff as a board. Didn't I take care of you just now? You feel like you got yourself primed and ready to fire all over again."

Seconds later, they were once more in the throes of coition.

When they fell apart this time, both shone with

sweat. They'd gone from a lustful hammering, to a slower tango, in which each was sorely aware of every inch of the carnal other, and then they'd risen to a howling, bed-squeaking crescendo before falling apart.

"You okay, hon?" Noxanne whispered.

Wilson took a moment to catch his breath and nodded. "You got a cold brew in the icebox?"

Noxanne's lips puckered, a spark of irritation in her eyes. Without a word, she rose and stalked naked into her mobile home's kitchen area and returned with two sweating beer bottles. For a while they drank in bed without speaking.

"You know," said Noxanne, "you still owe me for them two cases of beers."

Wilson shoved himself to an erect, Buddha-like sitting position, the bottle resting on his abdomen. Frowning, he took a swig. "What're you saying? You wanted to have this roll in the hay just to get me to pony up for them beers? Or is it you're just in the habit of getting money afterward?"

Noxanne turned and slapped him.

Wilson's eyes bugged and his mouth fell open. "Damn!" he said. "That smarts!"

"As well it should. You do think I'm a tramp, don't you?"

Wilson rubbed his jaw, which had turned a throbbing red. "Where in hellfire did you get all this tramp stuff from, anyway?"

Her eyes reddened and her chin began to tremble. "Where'd I get it? From your attitude, that's where I got it.

Why'd you have to bring up money like that?" She set her beer on the floor, slid prone, and began to bawl.

He started to writhe at the sound of her bawling. He took a long swig and set his bottle on the floor. "Okay, okay, I shouldn't of said what I did. It's just that ever woman I been with had ulterior motives. Seems like all they ever want is some kind of handout."

She quieted to blubbering. "I ain't that kind. I ain't. I had me some awkward relationships, and I do admit I took money from a man or two, but I never asked for it. They just offered to help me over one bad spot or another, so I took their money, and that was the end of it."

He reached for her. She pushed him away.

"Okay," he said, "I might've given you the impression I thought you was a skank, but as I think about it, it ain't the way I feel."

She rubbed one eye with a knuckle. "If you hadn't'a thunk it, you wouldn't'a said it."

"I didn't think it, sugar, I really didn't. It's just, well, doing the horizontal bop with you is better'n with any gal I ever been with." He reached for her again, and this time she didn't resist. He kissed her forehead and began stroking her hair again. "Some of the boys at Sam's do keep up that kind of talk, and some of it might rub off on a body's brain, but that ain't the way I think about you."

She jerked away, threw herself up onto one elbow. "Who? Who's been saying that stuff? It was Willie Pete and Worm, wasn't it? Or was it Melvin? 'Cause I swear, I'll

31

_"

He shushed her. Slowly, she reclined. He began nibbling at her ear. "It don't matter," he said. "It don't matter who said what. It's all talk, and that's all it is."

She turned her back to him and began to bawl into her pillow. "Y'all all think I'm trashy, but I ain't!"

Wilson muttered softly to himself. He sat up, reached for his beer, and finished it in one long gulp. "I don't think that, Noxanne, and that's the last time I'm telling you." He threw a leg across her and reached for her beer. He took a long, satisfying swig.

After a while, she stopped crying and pulled herself to a cross-legged sitting position facing him.

He offered the beer, and she took it. After she'd taken a couple of sips, he waggled the fingers of one hand, wanting it back. He drank deeply and again rested the bottle on his belly. "You okay now?" he asked.

Her chin fell to her chest. She nodded. He handed her the beer, rose, and took another from the refrigerator.

When he returned, he said, "I can pay you for them two cases of beers on Friday." He fidgeted as he stood before the bed. "We get paid in the afternoon. I'll go right to the bank and cash my check, and I don't care how long I got to stand in line to do it."

"It ain't that," she said. "You know it ain't."

His brow furrowed into a frown. "Well, what is, then? 'Cause you been making all kinds of accusations, and frankly I don't know what to make of it."

"Yes, you do, Wilson. You know exactly what to make of it."

His brow furrows grew deeper. He pawed the carpet before the bed. "Damn if I do. I ain't even close to having a clue."

She'd been picking at the label on her beer bottle. Now she snatched a long, slender piece from it, crumpled the paper with one hand, and threw it across the bedroom. "Okay, then," she said, "let me ask you this. And if you don't get it this time, you're just plain dumb."

He snickered. "Well, I ain't dumb, so out with it."

"I been wondering just how long it's gonna take you to get that divorce."

He took a step or two backwards, toward the bedroom door.

"You might as well sit back down, Wilson. We need to talk about things. Things between you and me."

He sat on the bed's edge.

"It ain't gonna be as bad as all that. I ain't gonna bite your head off."

"Yeah, well," he said, "that'll take some convincing."

"If you ain't gonna divorce Lurleen, then just come on out with it. I'm a big girl, I can take it."

Neither said a word for a while. The air conditioning came on, issuing its throaty whisper. Noxanne pulled the sheet up to her chin. She hugged her knees beneath its tent-like drape.

"It's over between Lurleen and me," said Wilson.

"I figured that. But that ain't what I want to know about."

"You want to know what's in it for you."

Noxanne blinked, and her head snapped back as if she'd been struck. Her face contorted. "Y'see? That's what I been talking 'bout. You don't care 'bout me. You bought into all that talk of me being a tramp." Her head slipped forward and her shoulders began to shake as she cried without sound.

He reached a hand, then withdrew it. He closed his eyes and sighed.

Between sobs Noxanne said, "You – you're just – typical. You don't care – about me – even a little."

"C'mon, sugar, that ain't so." He nudged himself closer to her.

Stifling the sobs, she said, "Don't you want to be married again, Wilson? Don't you want to be happy together with somebody?"

"Well, hell yeah, sugar, I for sure do. But –"

"But I'm a tramp and you have to think about being with me 'cause I'm such a tramp."

Wilson blew out an irritated breath. "That ain't so, damn it."

She turned reddened eyes on him. "Well, you same as said I *am,* a tramp. You let all that pool hall talk influence you. That's what you really think, ain't it?"

"God bless it, Noxanne, we done covered that. I don't think you're a tramp. I never did."

The Lynyrd Skynyrd ring tone on Wilson's cell phone began. He reached for his jeans, fished the phone out of a pocket, and peered at it.

"It's Lurleen, ain't it?"

"Yeah."

"Then go ahead and answer it. But you ain't gotta say where you are and what you been doing."

"The call ain't important, and neither is she. I don't want to talk to her no more."

"Go ahead and answer it. I got to use the potty and get cleaned up."

She rose and strode into the bathroom. He waited until he heard water running, and then he retrieved Lurleen's message and called her. The conversation began quietly. Then it turned loud and heated. Finally, it cooled to an officious, business-like tone. He closed the phone as Noxanne returned. She had wrapped a white terrycloth bathrobe around herself, its sash circumscribing the globe of her abdomen. She sat at the bed's end.

"You don't need to tell me a thing," she said. "It ain't none of my business anyway."

"Yeah, I do," said Wilson, "'cause it's news. Fact is, it's some big news."

"All right," said Noxanne, head bowed.

"The hell of it is," he went on, "I can't talk to that woman without getting my bowels in an uproar."

She looked up. "That's 'cause you still got feelings."

"No, it ain't, damn it. I just can't have a civil conversation with her, that's all."

"All right then, what's this big news?"

"It's the biggest news of all, but we had to have a big fuss-fight 'fore she come out with it. She's done hired a lawyer."

Noxanne gasped. "You don't mean it."

35

Wilson nodded. "I got to pay the legal fees and court costs, but we're going to get that divorce."

Noxanne's eyes bulged. "You don't mean it!"

"It's a fact," he said. "We still got to set a court date, but it'll be maybe in a month. Then it'll be all over but the shouting."

She clambered across the bed and threw her arms around him. "I'm so sorry, honeybunch. I mean, I'm sorry you got to go through a day in court and all."

"She done cleaned me out," he replied, "so it ain't no big deal."

She pushed away. "You mean you ain't happy 'bout it?"

He gave her a mildly exasperated look. "I mean I already done the giving and she's already done the getting. It's over 'cept the legal-ese."

"So are you happy with it? You are, ain't you?"

He allowed a smile. "Yeah. I'm happy about it."

She squealed and hugged him again, and pulled him on top of her.

He laughed. "Uh uh, sugar. I ain't got the juice for another go-round with you. You just about drained me dry already."

Laughing together, they sat up.

"So that brings up another subject," he said.

She put a wary hand to her mouth.

Noticing, he took the hand. "What I mean is, in a month or so I'll be free and easy." He looked down. "So I was wondering if, you know, maybe we ought to move in together."

Another squeal, and this time she kissed him. "Wilson Noonsocket, you are such a rascal! Of course you can move in with me. You just name the day and we'll do it."

This time it was he who pushed away. "Now, hold on, sugar. I got myself a problem there. It ain't a level playing field that way, y'know?"

"Oh, Wilson, I wouldn't ever hold that over your head. It'd be an even deal, just you and me."

Wilson studied her for a minute and then grinned. "You and me," he sang, "and baby makes three."

A concerned look – you might've even called it a look of shock – slipped across Noxanne's face. "What're you saying? You saying you want a baby?"

Wilson swallowed, his face blush red. "Well, sure. I wouldn't mind that, I wouldn't mind it even a little bit."

She huffed. "I can't have no babies," she said. "The doc tole me my tubes was plugged up, or some such."

"Well," he said, "I got a good job over at the paper mill, so I expect we can adopt one."

She huffed again. "You ain't hearing me right. I don't want no babies."

He swallowed. "For real?"

"That's for real. I ain't cut out for motherhood. I just ain't."

He turned away and began to dress.

"Where you going?" she asked.

"I think I'll go shoot some pool."

"You coming back after that?"

"I don't know. All this stuff with Lurleen and you fussing 'bout people calling you a tramp and not wanting a baby, well, it's a lot for this ol' brain. I need to do me some thinking." He started for the door. Then he turned, kissed her forehead, and left.

She listened until the clatter of his rusty Chevrolet had shrunk to silence, and then she dropped face first into her pillow, balled a fist, and began to pound the bed.

CHAPTER III

"I believe I'll just shoot some more pool," said Donnie.

Sam edged his chair a step closer to the heater. Before long he nodded off. Donnie continued to line his shots. Finally Sam woke and lumbered to the restroom. Returning, he drew a cupful of draft and selected a packaged sandwich from the small refrigerator behind the bar.

"It's almost noon," he said. "You hungry yet?"

"Thirsty's more like it."

Sam drew another cupful and handed it across.

Donnie licked at the foam and then took a long pull from the amber liquid. He eyed Sam. "Kind of sad, y'know?"

Sam turned to peer at him. "What is?"

"I ain't judging, and that's a fact. But lately you been looking like your dog's done up and died. The pity is, you ain't got nothing to your name 'cept that mangy ol' hound. A dog's good to have around, I guess, but they's just so much a dog can do for you."

"Least he's quiet some. He don't yap my ear off like you been doing."

Donnie chuckled. "Maybe you do need to spend time singing some hymns."

Sam said nothing. He finished eating, and as he turned toward the trashcan with the sandwich container, a scowl darkened his face. He eyed Donnie and began drumming his fingers on the bar's top. "I got my trailer," he said at last, "and my dog ain't dead. Anyway, I got this pool hall, so that's that."

FAMILY BUSINESS

The man dropped his hunting jacket over a wall peg and sauntered to the back end of the pool hall. Shirt stretched to fullness at the shoulders, he bent his tall frame over the bar and whacked its gleaming surface with a flatted hand. Sam pushed away from the day's newspaper and peered over his glasses.

"Shot and a beer," the man said in a booming voice. "Two times."

A flush of annoyance settled over Sam at the stranger's overly loud exuberance. "Two?"

The man scratched at his jaw line, where a pair of intersecting scars lay all but hidden by a week's worth of bristles. He nodded toward the door. "Me and my brother got us a big ol' deer this morning."

Sam eyed the front entrance as he poured the shots and drew the beers.

"Jeb'll be along directly," the man said. One hand dropped to his belt and began fingering the hilt of a broad-bladed skinning knife. "We gutted that ol' buck in the woods, but Jeb still wanted to cut off the hind quarters and slice up the shanks. We been doing that out yonder. Been at it a while, so we decided to cut the dust and celebrate a little. I left Jeb to watch the meat. Say, you got ice?"

41

Sam gave the man a sour look and nodded. He found it mildly insulting for a customer to imply the need to leave someone in his parking lot to guard the day's kill, but in truth he recognized the need for it. His pool hall was an outlier at the eastern boundary of Striven, a somber little town a twenty-minute drive off the Interstate, between Lake Martin and Opelika. An establishment often preached against in the town's four Baptist churches and its two Methodist ones and complained about once in a great while in the Church of Saints and Sinners. Dope peddlers, hookers, and contraband sellers occasionally tried to set up shop in Sam's parking lot. The local police rarely came in person, leaving Sam's Place to the State Patrol's random, bothersome visits. So Sam had learned to enforce his own version of the law, and for the most part he'd managed to keep middle Alabama's nefarious types – and the boldest of game robbers – at bay without the taint of police help.

He looked the man up and down. "Don't believe I know you."

"Macabee Waters," the man said, "but ever'body calls me Mac." He offered a hand, and Sam took it. "That deer we got was an ol' granddad," Waters went on. "Sixteen points. We measured his rack at thirty-some inches across."

Sam squinted, gave the man a slow, disbelieving headshake. "Don't think I ever seen one that size hereabouts."

Mac Waters threw back his whiskey and half the beer. "You want to see him?" He finished the beer, clattered the pint beer cup onto the bar, and strode, chest out, toward the door.

"You want that ice now?" Sam called out.

"Naw," said Mac. "C'mon. We won't be a minute."

Sam followed.

"What's up?" asked Donnie, one of the finest shooters ever to shark a game of eight ball at Sam's.

"Got a big ol' deer outside," Mac said. He beamed as he retrieved his coat. "Y'all come on out and see it if you got a mind to."

Donnie rolled his cue onto the table, and he and another half dozen shooters trooped out behind Sam and Mac. It was the week before Thanksgiving, an important time for hunters. Not many in the town of Striven could afford to serve up turkey on that day, or even a salted ham. Most would feast on game meat, venison more often than not. The less able hunters would serve rabbit, and a few others would make do with squirrel and dumplings, or maybe fish and hushpuppies. Thus, freshly sliced venison bestowed on everyone at Sam's the thought of a fine holiday meal.

The day had turned glisteningly warm. Sam shaded his eyes and peered past Mac to a rusty pickup and a scar-faced man. The man, one knee to the truck bed, was busy cutting at the deer's hindquarters. A dented camp cooler sat before him, lid open.

Mac pulled the cooler close and peered inside. The proud grin that had possessed him since he'd entered Sam's Place fell away. "Where's all them shank cuts?"

Jeb, who was a good bit shorter than his brother but just as beefy, didn't look up. He wiped the long-bladed knife on a pant leg, then made three slits in the deer's fur, peeled it back, and began slicing at the remaining flesh on the hind quarter.

"You hear me?" said Mac. "I said where's all them shank cuts? They ain't enough meat here to feed a five year-old. What you think I'm gonna have for Thanksgiving?"

This time Jeb wiped his blade on the deer's fur, made a few long strokes across a whetstone, and stood. "Nelda drove by," he said, "on her way back from Wal-Mart. She saw me and so I had her take them cuts home."

Mac's eyes narrowed.

"Better part of that meat's mine," said Jeb. "That was our deal, if you remember."

Archie, a deep-voiced string bean customer of Sam's, pointed to Jeb. "I know that ol' boy. I seen him on the TV. He got sent up. Burglary, I believe it was."

A hum of voices.

"He didn't burgle nobody around here," said Donnie. "We ain't had no break-ins in years."

"It was over in Montgomery, where we used to live," said Mac. His glare remained fixed on Jeb. "When he got out of jail, we moved Mama and our women and kids here so's we could live a little bit cheaper."

"What'd he do?" someone asked.

"He broke into his own lawyer's house," said Mac. "The Good Lord never did give him the sense a 'possum might have."

Jeb's face flushed, highlighting the web of scars on his cheeks and forehead. He stood and waggled his butcher knife. "I did my time," he said. "I made amends."

Mac eyed Sam, then jabbed a finger at the deer carcass. "And yet you see what he done. He stole my meat."

Jeb's jaw worked back and forth. He jumped to the ground. "I shot that deer. I said you could have some of it, but them shanks is mine."

Sam studied the two, eyed Jeb's knife and the growing crowd of onlookers. He edged from the throng, pulling Archie with him. "This might come to nothing," he whispered, "but get back inside. If I give you the high sign, call the police."

Archie backed away and made for the pool hall.

"I saw that deer first," said Mac. "I pointed him out."

"Yeah, but I shot it," Jeb yelled. "That gives me rights."

In a blur, Mac threw his jacket to the ground, thumbed open the sheath at his belt, pulled out the skinning knife, and flicked the blade at Jeb's cheek, x-ing an existing scar.

Sam lurched into the space between the two brothers and shoved them apart. "Now don't even think about it, you two." He faced the shorter man. "Your brother ordered you a drink, and it's sitting on the bar right now." He turned to Mac. "So put them blades away. Come on inside and cool down."

Mac shoved Sam. Caught unawares, Sam fell in a heap.

Jeb bellowed, made a downward pass with the butcher knife. The sleeve above his brother's knife hand fluttered open and blood coursed. Mac winced. A rain-spatter of blood began to gather at his feet. Mac slipped the knife to his other hand.

Sam rose with the help of a pair of bystanders and waved to Archie, who disappeared inside. The two brothers slowly circled.

"Ever'body get outta the way!" Sam yelled. He began pushing at the onlookers.

Jeb swung his knife again and danced away, agile as a boxer. Mac's shirt opened at the waist. His abdomen showed a pink welt, but only a trickle of blood. Jeb swung the butcher knife again and missed. Mac caught Jeb's wrist with his bloody hand and made a sideways swipe with the skinning knife. A red sea gushed from Jeb's armpit, a thin layer of adipose curling outward on both sides of the cut. His plaid shirt darkened to a sodden red.

Archie ran to Sam. "I called 'em," he said. "The chief cussed a blue streak, but he said they'd be here soon's they could saddle up."

Sam shook his head. "This ain't good. This ain't good at all."

Sunlight caught the brothers' blades as they continued to circle and slash, each knife stroke scribing long, shimmering arcs in the space between them. Then another pass of Jeb's blade cut deep into Mac's abdomen. Mac stumbled into the crowd. The onlookers retreated.

"Lord, no!" said a woman, she and her husband out-of–staters who had pulled into the parking lot to scan a map. She buried her face in her husband's shoulder.

An old Chevy Malibu pulled off the highway, stereo blaring. The driver revved his engine, flung up a double line of gravel, and plunged the car into a space alongside Sam's building. Doors flew open. Five boys burst from the car, laughing and elbowing.

Sam thrust a finger at them. "The police are coming," he called out. "If any one of you adds to this fuss, I'll have 'em haul you in."

The boys backed away.

Mac and Jeb had been orbiting at the crowd's core, preoccupied with their wounds, a bloody oval on the gravel tracing their movement. Jeb stopped at the mention of police. He glanced contritely at Sam. "You see these scars?" he said, pointing to his face. "He done this to me."

"Shut up," said Mac. Another flick caught Jeb over one eye.

Jeb blinked, shook his head, sending a spray of sweat and blood into the crowd.

"I got you now," said Mac. "You ain't gonna run to Mama this time."

A faint whine grew to a howl on the road from Striven. A police car hove into view, cleaving the sunny day with arcs of red light.

Jeb dodged Mac's lunge and cut a furrow in his brother's shoulder.

Two policemen leaped to the gravel, the first one clenching a blackjack, the other a nightstick. The first one shoved in, swung his blackjack at Mac. Jeb cursed the cop, kicked at him, then lunged at the second. He sliced the policeman's club arm, dyeing his khaki uniform sleeve a deep crimson.

Mac had fallen with the blackjack's glancing blow. He clambered to his feet and butted the first cop, who again raised the blackjack.

"No!" said Sam. He grabbed the cop's arm, pulled him from the crowd, held him there. The cop struggled, but Sam's strength was greater.

"You hit at one like that after this much blood," said Sam, "and the other'll always come after you."

The policeman eyed his partner, took in his wound. He dashed for the patrol car and a first aid kit.

"Hey, scarface!" one of the five boys hooted from their car. "Cut 'em again!" His cronies howled their agreement.

A second police car bounded into Sam's parking lot and swerved to a stop. Wayman Tucker, Striven's chief of police, pushed his pudgy frame to the gravel from the rider's side. Sam left the crowd to meet him.

"What got this going?" Tucker asked.

Sam nodded toward the truck. "They got to jawing about who gets what off that deer."

Tucker glanced to his wounded officer, the other wrapping the arm cut with a long bandage. Then Tucker eyed the two circling brothers. "Hell, I got to stop this." He shoved into the crowd.

Sam grabbed at the chief's arm, missed. "You can't," he called out. "You'll just get pulled in."

Mac flicked his blade. Blood spread across Tucker's broad chest.

The chief stumbled back. He touched the cut, then looked to Sam. "This is on your property, and you ain't controlling it."

Sam grunted. "Things get to a point, they ain't no controlling it."

"Then why the hell'd you call me in?"

Sam stiffened. "Law needs to be here, I reckon, for what that's worth."

Tucker glared. "Then I'm gonna cite you for letting this get started." He glanced to his cut. "And for putting the law in jeopardy like that."

Sam spat at the chief's feet.

The brothers were stumbling now, their clothes a canvas of tatters and ballooning stains. Their cuts yawned wide, exposing slashed muscles and pink bone. Jeb's cut eyebrow flopped, flag-like. Below it, a clot had begun to jut. One arm hung limp against its gashed armpit. Mac's cut shoulder slumped, the arm dangling, its strength gone. A tube of intestines peeked from his abdomen.

Donnie glanced to Sam, then to Tucker. "You ain't gonna do nothing? These two gonna kill each other."

The chief and his two policemen had turned slack-jawed and rapt as the fight continued. The cop with the cut arm eyed Donnie and shook his head.

"Hey!" one of the boys yelled. "Somebody cut somebody!" His friends took up the taunt.

Sam turned to the boys. "Shut up!" He turned back, pawing the ground with a boot toe and mumbling to nobody in particular.

"Jesus," Tucker said, suddenly awake from his trance, "I can't stand here and watch them boys snuff each other out."

"They're slowing down," said Sam. "Maybe they had their fill of it."

The brothers made ever-weaker passes with their blades. The crowd quieted.

Suddenly Jeb staggered forward. He plunged his knife into his brother's chest. As the blade hit bone, he lost his footing. The knife jerked down, opening a long, wavering path into Mac's abdomen. Freshly cut muscles wriggled like live wires. Mac dropped to his knees.

The chief turned to his approaching driver. "Willis, call Doc Quincey, see if he can break loose. Step on it, now!"

Willis raced off.

"That deer's mine," Jeb gasped.

Mac didn't look up. "You can have it," he croaked.

Jeb slumped against the tailgate, drooling blood. He looked to the crowd. "You heard him, didn't you? That deer's mine."

"Yeah," someone said. "It's yours, fair and square."

"Think you're better," Mac gasped. "Just 'cause you got a mama."

Jeb spat a long string of blood. "'Dopted bastard."

Mac pushed himself to his feet. "Gonna kill you." He rose, teetering.

"You ain't," said Jeb. He tested the butcher knife's edge with his thumb.

Mac slurred, "Son of a bitch." He staggered, his knife slashing.

"He's gonna fall!" someone said.

Mac lunged for his brother. A slight pop sounded as Jeb's blade disappeared into Mac's chest. The two came together. Jeb turned wild-eyed as they fell to the ground. Mac rolled away, his stubby knife like a monument in Jeb's chest. A pink bubble appeared on Mac's lips. He groaned, issued a final breath, and went limp.

Sam dropped to his knees and bent over Jeb. "We called the doctor, son. You hang on, you hear? He'll be here in a minute."

"Hurt," said Jeb.

"I know," said Sam. "It must hurt awful bad."

"Here," said Jeb, holding a quaking hand to his heart.

"You just hold on best you can," said Sam.

"He dead?" said Jeb.

Sam glanced to Mac's still body. "'Fraid so."

Jeb's arms and legs spasmed. He groaned as the gravel ground into his back. "Going to hell," he mumbled, "Killed my brother."

"He had as big a hand in this as you," said Sam. He pulled the knife from Jeb's chest. The lung's puncture frothed and announced a faint, bubbling whistle.

"Straight to hell," Jeb muttered.

51

The boys had left their car and joined the crowd, as if pulled there by magnet force. They stared at the two mutilated bodies, their faces drawn and penitent.

A car drove up, parked next to the boys' Chevy. A tall picket of a man climbed out, a medical bag in his hand. "All right," he said in a deep, cigarette-hoarsened voice. "What's been going on here?" He shoved in until he stood before Sam and the two brothers.

"Knife fight," said one bystander.

"Never saw nothing like it," said another.

"Killed each other," said yet another.

Sam looked up, a scowl pressing new folds into his fleshy face. "Give Doc Quincey some room!" he yelled. Then quieter: "And have a little respect for the two on the ground."

Doc Quincey pressed a finger to Jeb's neck. "Why didn't someone stop this?"

"I tried," said Tucker, now holding a soggy wad of gauze to his cut. "They wouldn't have any of it."

Sam set a hand on Jeb's chest. "I guess you could say this one finished it."

The doctor fingered open one of Jeb's eyes. Jeb squirmed feebly with the surge of light.

"He won't make it," said Quincey. "Pulse is too weak. He's lost too much blood."

Jeb sighed and expired.

"He's gone?" Sam asked.

Quincey looked up. "Yes."

Sam picked up Mac's hunting jacket and draped it over Jeb's head. Then he rose, eyes sparking as he looked to each face in the crowd. "I guess you all got an eyeful, huh?"

A wave of mumbles passed through the onlookers.

"You see what happens?" Sam said. "It ain't exactly the sporting affair you figured it for, now is it? Hellfire, folks, nobody wins a fight like this."

Tucker broke a long silence. "I still got to cite you," he said to Sam. "Get on inside so I can write you up proper."

Sam kicked at the gravel. "I tole you, law don't work in this sort of sit'ation." He turned again to the crowd. "I'm closing up shop for a few days, so get on home." He lumbered toward the steps to his place. Tucker lurched along behind, blood from the soaked wad of gauze dripping from his fingers. Quincey followed.

When the door had closed behind the three, a man in the crowd pointed to the bodies and said, "They wasn't brothers. Not really."

"They was," said Donnie. "Don't you know nothing? They killed each other over a deer. A dang deer! If they wasn't brothers, do you think they'd of carried it that far?"

CHAPTER IV

Donnie didn't look up. "Sometimes I got to look after more'n the here and now, that's all I'm saying."

"Bull," said Sam. "You just get scared Hell's gonna scorch your britches. Then you let them sons of bitches twist you ever which way." Sam waggled his fingers for Donnie's beer cup. He refilled it and handed it back. "Myself, I ain't been much on religion since I come back from the 'Nam, 'specially the kind of gospel they spew around here."

Donnie probed the gap in his lower teeth with his tongue. He frowned. Then he shrugged and sipped his beer.

Sam snorted. "You think you can have it both ways, don't you? You think you can chase women and gamble, drink and carouse, and then you can run off to church, and you won't stay up nights worrying 'bout what's gonna happen to you when you die. Worse yet, you let that ol' preacher and his deacons lord it over you – until you get tired of it, that is. Then you thumb your nose at 'em and waltz on down the road and don't give a thought to whether they'll take you back next time you feel the need for a little religion."

Donnie backed up to his table. Sam was becoming a scold, and Donnie didn't like it. "It ain't exactly like that. It ain't, Sam, and you know it."

"Okay, let me ask you, then. Just what do you get outta Sunday mornings hollering them hymns and amen-ing ever other thing that comes outta Wesley Wilding's mouth?"

54

Donnie threw back his beer, crumpled the plastic cup, and tossed it in the general direction of the trashcan. "I'm going back to shooting pool."

DONNIE'S DECISION

The Wimple home, at the corner of Chester and Willard, near the easternmost city limit of Striven, had once been a clean, well-kept place. Being homebodies, Buster and his wife Bunny had opted to spend their extra money on embellishing the home and quarter acre lot instead of on travel, mail-order clothes, and cars; thus the home had become something of a showpiece in the Alabama town. But then Buster grew ill. Bunny had to quit work to tend to her husband, and the house and yard deteriorated. Finally, a stroke completed the work Buster's Parkinson's disease had begun five years earlier.

The day of the funeral, son Donnie helped Bunny to the front curb and into the family's now-shabby Ford Escort. He took his place at the wheel. As the car's engine groaned to life and began its labors, Bunny placed a hand on her son's arm and motioned for him to turn the engine off.

"The house," she said, "just look at it."

He killed the engine and looked. The porch developed a noticeable sag. Paint flaked everywhere on the siding. A gutter hung by a thread on the house's left side, which faced Willard Avenue. The front yard that Buster had kept as meticulously as a golf course had become a scattering of weeds and bare dirt. The shrubs were overgrown, Bunny's flowerbeds mounded with moldy leaves from the lot's aged sycamore.

"It don't look like much," said Donnie.

"It *doesn't* look like," said Bunny.

He scowled. "Awright, but you know I don't care about all that school stuff. And 'sides, you ain't a schoolteacher no more. So what's the big deal about the house?"

Bunny sighed. "A family's home always seems to represent what's going on inside, you know? When your father had his health and I had my work, everything seemed to click for us. We kept the place looking like a million."

"Okay," Donnie drawled, mouth pursed.

"Don't you see, son? It's as if the house became ill, too." She wiped away a tear. "Donald, I'm so deep in debt. What am I going to do?"

He reached, pulled her gaunt body to him. "Ever'thing's gonna be just fine, Mama. I'm gonna go on the road shooting pool and make lots of money. We'll fix that ol' house up 'til it shines like a new dime."

But as the months passed, everything wasn't fine. Donnie had developed into a decent shooter, and he did go on the road, but the gamers out there picked him clean. So he tucked his tail and slunk back home. He gave Bunny what money he could from his winnings at Sam's Place, but that, along with the sum she made tutoring high school football players, was barely enough to keep their heads above water.

Then Donnie had his moment of pool-shooting

glory – tainted though it turned out to be – at the expense of an air conditioning salesman from Georgia. The man had flounced his shiny, new Expedition off the highway and into Sam's parking lot late one morning and, with a couple of hours to kill, he ordered up a beer and a sandwich and began shooting pool alone at a table near the bar.

Donnie had been nursing a late morning beer. He turned to watch the tall, overweight man line his shots. After a while, his studied frown rose to a grin. "Them's some fine shots you been making," he called out.

The man glanced up, brushed at his bushy gray hair, looked Donnie up and down, and nodded. "I'm a little rusty," he said, "but I'm feeling lucky. Want a game?"

Donnie laced his fingers together, bent them outward until the joints crackled. "What you got in mind?"

"I always favor a game of rotation," the man said.

Donnie stuffed the sneer he felt coming. Rotation, with its fifteen balls, made for a busy table, and that could only benefit green players on a lucky roll. But he'd seen enough of this man's shooting to realize his lack of finesse. He'd play this fellow, and he'd beat him out of whatever he had in his wallet. "Okay by me," he replied. "Lag for break?"

The man declined and offered Donnie the opening break.

Donnie played inconsistently at first; that was the way he'd always lined his pockets – he'd miss a shot here and there, keep his opponent encouraged, then nudge the bets upward. But this man's shots were falling in cascades, and he began thinning Donnie's roll of twenties. A half hour later, Donnie decided he'd better quit the cute stuff and really play. He slowly began to recoup his losses. Their bets – and the crowd about them – began to grow.

Finally, the man backed away, opened his wallet wide, and canted it so Donnie could see its now-barren fold. "I-I'm out of cash. Any way you can take a credit card?"

Donnie chortled. "What d'you take me for, a cashier from over at the Wal-Mart? If you ain't got no more cash, then we're done."

The man licked his lips. His eyelids twitched. "I can get cash at the downtown bank."

Donnie thought a minute, and then strode to the front door and peered out. "That black Expedition's yours, ain't it?"

The man nodded. He began to mouth-breathe.

"What amount you see us betting? If we keep playing, that is."

"Oh, a hundred a game, easily. Maybe more."

Donnie bit his bottom lip as he pretended to consider that. "Tell you what. We'd likely keep at this all afternoon, but I got to be somewhere in an hour or so. So I'm thinking we could sum it all up right now by playing for that Expedition."

The man's chin trembled. "My car?"

Donnie propped one boot on a pair of Coke crates stacked near the door. "You look like a straight-up fellow, so I'm gonna give you a chance to get all your money back, against that car. One game." He grinned. "How's that for a bet?"

Donnie expected the man to laugh at his proposition, but he didn't. Instead, the man trotted to his SUV, returned, and slapped the title to the tabletop.

Donnie's grin broadened. He nodded. The salesman broke. Sam's customers had begun calling friends as the games had progressed, and now the table had a crowd three deep.

Donnie couldn't miss, and the game was quickly over. He rolled his stick onto the felt tabletop.

The man blubbered as he signed the title paper and pushed it across to Donnie. The crowd began to dissipate. Donnie pressed the title into his shirt pocket, put his arm around the man, walked him to the bar, and bought him a beer. The cold, foaming brew seemed to fortify the man, and his blubbering stopped. "Can you drive me to Montgomery?" he asked of Donnie. "I have a sales meeting there I can't miss."

So Donnie drove him to Montgomery. Returning, he pulled to the curb in front of the house and honked. When he saw Bunny peering through the screened door, he honked again and waved for her to come out.

She took in the car from the front porch and then strode toward him, wagging a finger. "Donald, we don't have money for this. You're going to have to take it back."

Donnie guffawed. "I didn't buy it, Mama, and in case you got your mind on it, I didn't steal it, neither."

She jabbed bony fists into her hips and sighed. "Have," she said. "*Have* your mind on it. And *neither* is wrong usage."

He ignored the grammar lesson. "I *won* it, Mama. I won it off some salesman at Sam's."

She seemed about to say something more; instead, she shook her head and plodded back into the house.

Donnie frowned at that, sighed, and then he shrugged it off and drove around town, honking at friends. After a while, he drove to the outskirts of town, on the Montgomery Highway, and pulled onto the shoulder. His coup was beginning to make him nervous. Had he done something illegal in taking the man's ride? He turned and drove slowly back to town.

Sure enough, a police car and two Montgomery deputy sheriffs were waiting for him at the curb. Donnie pulled up behind the police car and got out.

"You here about this Expedition, I expect."

"That's right," said the first deputy, a wiry man with bulging arms.

"I won it fair and square from that salesman fellow," said Donnie. He pulled out the title and opened it for the policeman to see the signatures. "That game was honest as the day is long," he added.

The policeman reached for the paper. Donnie pulled it out of reach. He showed the signatures to the second policeman, a tall, thin, intent-looking man.

The first policeman waved a writ at Donnie. "Sorry buddy," he said, "we have to impound the car until the judge holds a hearing."

Donnie's lips wrinkled beneath a furrowed brow. "That ain't worth two shits."

"I know," said the first deputy. "It's not the sort of

work we signed up for, but I can tell you unofficially that the burden of proof is on this man, Mr. Winton Evinrude, to prove there was something crooked in the deal."

Donnie looked to his boots and blew out a breath. "When's this hearing?"

"It's on the writ," said the deputy. "Here's your copy."

The other deputy held out a hand for the title and Donnie's keys, climbed into the SUV, and followed the police car toward Montgomery.

The hearing was held on a Wednesday, two days after the impound. Bunny's Ford Escort, which now seemed on its last legs, carried mother and son to the Montgomery courthouse. *You got to go, Mama*, Donnie had told Bunny, *'cause if they give me the car back, you got to drive the Escort home. Donald*, she'd replied, *you know I don't feel comfortable driving that old car. That's awright, Mama, you just foller me. I'll drive slow and keep an eye on you.*

The courtroom was located in a blocky-looking building in downtown Montgomery. Inside, light flooded the high-ceilinged space from a row of elongated vertical windows, the room strangely quiet, quieter even than the sanctuary of the United Methodist Church of Greater Striven, where Donnie spent an occasional Sunday morning. Winton Evinrude sat on the front row with his lawyer.

"That's him, Mama," Donnie whispered. "That's the sumbitch I won the car off of."

Bunny took in the salesman and then whispered, "Nothing's ever been gained by the use of profanity,

Donald. And you won the car *from* this man."

Donnie didn't reply. He guided Bunny across the aisle to the front row opposite Evinrude and his lawyer.

Minutes later, a man in uniform entered and bade the courtroom's scattered occupants to stand. The judge strode in, a short, mocha-skinned man with a Brillo pad of hair hovering about his head like an aura. The uniformed man announced Donnie's hearing.

The judge pored over a paper the uniformed man handed him, and then he looked to Donnie. "Mr. Wimple, are you represented by counsel?"

"He means a lawyer," Bunny whispered.

Donnie stood. "No, sir, Judge. I just come to get my car back."

The judge sniffed and turned to Evinrude. His lawyer, a handsome man in an expensive, tailored suit, stood.

The judge said, "I have a title here signed by both Mr. Wimple and Mr. Evinrude. What exactly is your complaint?"

"Our contention is that Mr. Wimple is a pool shark, Your Honor, a bottom feeder, preying on the unsuspecting. A two-bit hustler of dubious intentions."

"Hey!" said Donnie, "I ain't no two-bit —"

"Hush!" the judge said. "I'll get to you in a minute." He turned again to Evinrude's lawyer. "Before Mr. Wimple's character becomes relevant, your client will have to convince me something irregular occurred in the signing of this title."

"Exactly right, Your Honor. Mr. Wimple

manipulated a contest of rotation pool to his benefit. He preyed on my client, as hustlers will, and finally conned him into signing over the Expedition as restitution for his bets."

Donnie protested, and Evinrude's lawyer raised an objection, their voices rising with each word. The judge shushed them. He turned to Donnie. "All right, Mr. Wimple, what's your version of how this change of ownership came to pass?"

Donnie, now edgy as a cornered cat, stammered and rambled, but he finally completed his story. A moment of silence, and then he added, "When I look back on it, Judge, I think he's got a gambling problem. I think he's hooked on games. Seems to me he can't stop betting. If I didn't want his car real bad, I'd of give it back to him and tole him to give up on games."

Evinrude's lawyer said, "Then Mr. Wimple realized my client was, and had been, in an emotional state, Your Honor. He'd had some romantic ups and downs, and he wasn't himself that day."

Donnie had sat, but now he bolted upright. "Judge, I'm just a pool shooter. I know how to hustle, but that ain't no crime. I seen used car dealers do it every day, real bidness people, too, and even a lawyer or two. 'Sides, they ain't no way a pool shooter can size up a body beforehand as to whether he's had any nooky lately."

A wave of titters passed through the courtroom. Bunny sighed. The judge stifled a smile and admonished Donnie to watch his language. Donnie reddened, head bowed.

"All right," said the judge, "it seems to me that Mr. Wimple did take advantage of Mr. Evinrude."

"Hey!" Donnie said.

"Not a word, Mr. Wimple. Not a single word. Sit."

Donnie sat.

"However," the judge went on, "from both Mr. Evinrude's version and Mr. Wimple's, it seems Mr. Evinrude's emotional state was beside the point. His weakness for gambling was clearly to blame for his loss of the car."

A clamor rose from Evinrude and his lawyer, and Donnie turned a grin to his mother. "Hot dang!" he yelled in triumph. The judge gaveled them all to silence.

"However, Mr. Wimple," the judge said, "if I ever see you in my courtroom again, I won't be as benevolent."

On the way back to Striven, Donnie could barely keep his foot from flattening the accelerator pedal, but he managed to guide Bunny slowly back home. Then he made the rounds of Striven, once again honking and yelling. At Sam's, Archie and Wilson bought him drinks until midnight, when Sam closed up shop. By then, Donnie was so looped that Sam had to let him sleep it off on a cot behind the bar.

The next morning, as Sam opened the pool hall's front door, he called out, "The powder's in that pasteboard box on the shelf under the cash register. Get yourself some."

Donnie fumbled through the box until he found a packet of Stanback powder, drew a cupful from the tap, and stirred the analgesic into his beer with a forefinger. He tipped the cup and hungrily swallowed.

"What you gonna do with that big ol' SUV?" Sam asked.

"Drive it around, I expect," said Donnie. "Same as I would Mama's car. Why?" He rubbed at his red-veined eyes and then attempted to massage the previous night from his temples.

"That sort of vehicle, it just don't seem to fit you, that's all."

Donnie blinked until Sam came into full focus. "Maybe I'm changing my ways."

"Like you did last night?"

"That don't count. I was cel'brating."

"Uh huh."

Donnie climbed back into the Expedition and drove home. He mounted the porch and opened the front door. His mother was crying. She held up a letter the postman had just delivered. Donnie took it and slumped into his recliner. His temples still thumped malevolently, and it took a couple of minutes for him to read the brief letter. An outstanding bill for Buster's care during his final days had accrued a mass of late charges. The hospital had been sending bills for over a year, but Bunny could never manage to pay, and now the hospital administration had enlisted a collection agency. A bill collector was to come the next afternoon.

Donnie sighed. "What you gonna do, Mama?"

She daubed at her eyes with a wadded tissue, and then blew her nose. "That depends on you, Donald."

He swallowed. "Me?"

"You were going to give me a little something each month for room and board."

"I did, Mama, don't you 'member?"

She drew herself up to a rigid posture. "That was four months ago. Since then, son, you've been carousing and gambling, and you haven't given me a penny."

"Aw, Mama."

"Here's what it comes down to," she said. "I have two hundred or so saved that I can put toward the debt. That should keep the hospital at bay for another month. But the only way I can make more payments on the bill depends on you."

Donnie swallowed again.

"Either you come up with some money to help out, or I'm going to have to ask you to move out."

"Move out? Mama, where'll I go?"

"That's up to you, Donald."

The ultimatum had a sobering effect. He pushed himself to his feet. "I got me an idea," he said. He stuffed the letter into a shirt pocket and stalked from the house.

He came home late that night – sober. The next morning, he left before Bunny rose. When he returned that afternoon, Bunny was sitting on the couch, the bill collector in Donnie's recliner.

Donnie glared and then turned to Bunny. "Don't give 'em a dang dime, Mama."

The man rose, frowning.

Donnie pulled a cashier's check from his shirt pocket and handed it to the man. "I b'lieve the bill was for this much, according to that dang letter."

The man looked at the check, then to Donnie. He nodded, his frown easing. "To the penny."

"It's made out all proper and ever'thing, ain't it?"

The man nodded and put the check in his briefcase. He shook Donnie's hand, then Bunny's, and he left.

Bunny gave her son a stern look. "Donald Abraham Wimple, where did you get that money?"

He chuckled. "Come look out the front door."

She took his hand.

"I made a deal over in Auburn for the Expedition. A car like that's pop'lar with them college high rollers, so I got a pretty penny for it. Then this morning, I got Archie to take me to Opelika, where this truck was for sale. That ol' boy had a pull-along camper for sale, too, and the truck's got some mileage on it, so I put my best hustle on 'em and got 'em both for a song." He pulled another check from his shirt pocket, this one for nineteen hundred, and he handed it to Bunny.

"So now I ain't gotta move. I can stay here with you, Mama, forever and ever."

Anger fled across Bunny's face, and then a look of defeat emerged. She returned to the couch and slumped into its back.

Donnie had been grinning proudly, but now his grin faded.

He sat beside her, put a spindly arm about her spare frame. "Mama, ain't you happy? You got that debt off you, and some more to boot."

She rubbed her eyes, took his hand, and forced a

strained smile. "Thank, you, Donald. I don't know how I'd have paid that bill otherwise."

Donnie studied her. "Then what's got you down in the mouth?"

She patted his hand and let go. "You'll never change, will you, son?"

He studied her again for a moment. Then the grin returned. He chucked her under the chin. "No'm, I s'pose not."

CHAPTER V

A half hour passed. Sam readied a new keg for the tap. He wiped down the bar and made a few swipes at the dusty floorboards with his broom. He took out the trash and burned it. When he returned, Donnie was absently whistling as he filled another cup.

"All right, then," said Sam, "let me ask you one more time. If Wesley Wilding and that church bunch of his is so all-fired important to you, then what do you get from hanging out with 'em?"

Donnie sniffed, worked his mouth back and forth as if chewing. "I like singing. I get to sing a little bit."

"That ain't much of a answer," said Sam.

Donnie began an awkward shuffling.

Sam smirked. "That's what I thought. You just hide out there when you think them sins've been mounting up and they about to tumble all over you."

Donnie stomped a boot, sending a thunderclap through the rafters. "Dang it, Sam, what's crawled up your ass this morning?"

Sam leaned, arms braced on the bar. "Just tell me, has all that done you any good?"

Donnie sighed. "Not according to Mama."

"And she should know," Sam said, as if it were a question.

Donnie nodded. "She's the smartest person I ever knowed."

WHAT MIGHT'VE BEEN

"Hey, Sam!"

The proprietor of Striven's only pool hall looked up from the beer keg he'd just finished tapping and turned toward Archie's booming voice.

"You remember Travis Wilhite, I bet."

Sure, Sam remembered Travis. They'd been drafted, back in 'sixty-nine, Travis number ten in the Selective Service lottery, Sam Witherspoon eighteenth. They'd both been working at the Bradstreet paper mill when their numbers were called, and they'd ridden the bus together to Fort Benning for boot camp. They'd remained at Benning for advanced infantry training, and together they'd climbed aboard a military transport plane bound for Vietnam.

Archie leaned one of Sam's rickety, cane-bottom chairs against the wall, his long legs kicked out over an upturned Coke crate. He held that morning's copy of the *Montgomery Advertiser* at arm's length; he'd been glancing at pictures, now running his finger under the name he could barely read. "It's him, sure 'nough."

Sam reached under the bar, pulled out his own copy. He followed his finger down the obit's right-hand column and read the first paragraph.

> **Wilhite, Travis Daniel** –
> After a heroic battle with
> cancer, Travis Daniel Wilhite
> surrendered his soul to the
> arms of our Lord on
> December 18. He is survived
> by wife Lora and two sons,
> Travis Junior and Carter
> Ephram Wilhite. Services will
> be held at Gossett Funeral
> Home on December 21st at 1
> p.m.

"I bet he was having a time of it," said Archie. "I heard Agent Orange got into him."

Sam looked at the Pabst Blue Ribbon clock on the rear wall. A few minutes past ten. He'd had a mere handful of customers since the weekend, and might not have any today, this close to Christmas.

"Can you tend the place for me this afternoon?" he asked. "I'm going to the funeral."

Archie nodded. "Didn't know you and him was that good a friends."

"We was, once," said Sam.

"Okay, then," said Archie. "Gimme the keys."

"Pull a couple of beers off that new keg," Sam said. "Sandwiches are in the fridge if you want one."

Archie grinned. "Hey, awright."

Sam tossed him the keys and left.

His suit coat ripped at a shoulder seam as he twisted himself free of his pickup's cab. He'd always been a bulky person, but the torn coat told him he'd gained weight since summer. He took off the coat, tossed it inside, shut the truck door, and made his way through angled lines of parked cars to the funeral home sanctuary.

Travis. His old comrade, the loud, beer-swilling man Sam had haunted saloons and whorehouses with in Thailand. The cancer had apparently shrunken him to nothing before he died. The corpse hardly resembled the man as Sam had last seen him. They'd had a falling out that day, not long after their return to civilian life. Sam had lain around for a couple of months prior, trying to shove the war to the back of his mind, meanwhile ignoring Lora, the girlfriend he'd left behind when he'd boarded the plane for Nam. Then he'd dragged himself back to the paper mill and a supposedly waiting job. There, he'd discovered, Travis had quickly gone back to work, had impressed the supervisor with his industry, and had used that bit of influence to get Lora's brother Jackson on in Sam's place.

Had to do it, Travis had replied when Sam confronted him at the plant's front entrance. *Me and Lora got together soon's I was discharged, but she said she couldn't get married until Jack had a job. He'd been drinking off and on since high school, and she thought the job would be good for him.*

That had stung. Sam and Lora had been dating for a couple of years before boot camp, and they'd more or less planned to marry when he returned from his tour of duty in Vietnam. Or, he'd thought as he stood toe to toe

73

with Travis that day at the paper mill, *maybe I just assumed she was all hepped up to marry me.* After all, Sam had never been the most demonstrative man in Alabama, and his romantic skills weren't exactly legendary. *You know we was writing each other,* Sam had replied to Travis. *Yeah, but you quit writing,* Travis had replied. *She thought you give up on her.*

Sam hadn't; it was the war, remembering the long weeks in the bush, the days of sleeping off his exhaustion when they returned to base camp, then more days of sleeping off his hangovers after drowning the boredom of base camp routine in free beer and whiskey. It had been crazy – when he was in the bush, all he could think about was getting back to base camp. Then, back at base camp, remembering the adrenalin charge of firefights had constantly pulled him to the firebase's barbed wire to peer into the jungle for any hint of action. He hadn't meant to put Lora on the back burner like that, but there it was – staring him in the face that day – Travis and Lora about to marry.

He'd decked Travis, right there in front of the paper mill office, and had strode off before anyone could call the cops. He'd taken a job sweeping out his uncle's pool hall for a buck-fifty an hour, and had stayed on until the uncle died, the old man's will awarding the place to Sam. That had been that. No family, no retirement, no benefits, and very little time off. Just that old pool hall. Travis had gone around for a month with stitches in a puffy mouth and jaw, or so Sam had heard. Then, after Travis and Lora moved to Montgomery, Sam had lost track of them both.

The embalmed body still showed a scar where Sam had mangled Travis' face with that haymaker punch. He reached a hand toward the scar tissue's ridge, then drew back, still embarrassed at his compulsion to touch corpses, a tic he'd developed during his tour of duty. He turned, whispered something to Lora – moments later he couldn't remember what – and he took his seat.

After the service, he waited until he could catch her alone outside.

"I'm real sorry," he said, coatless and fighting off shivers from a northwest wind. "It was that Agent Orange, wasn't it?"

Lora nodded. "Why'd you come, Sam?"

He looked away, trying to put words to the empty feeling that had been eating away at his insides for decades. "Guess the news had me looking back at old times," he said.

"He talked about you a lot," said Lora. "He'd have a few beers, and he'd start telling me about something or other over there. He'd mention you, and then he'd stop. I'd ask him more about it, and he'd clam up."

"I never did get over you up and marrying him like that," said Sam. "I was young, and I reckon I was about as dumb as a young fellow can be. I just been wishing lately that we'd of ended it proper, that's all."

Lora looked away, as if peering into her own inner void.

"Look," said Sam, "I know this ain't the time or place, but I was just thinking maybe you and me could have dinner sometime."

"Why, Sam?"

Hell's bells, he thought, the why of that was obvious. For years, Lora had crept into his thoughts when he'd least expected it. He needed to get over it, and maybe she did, too.

She cocked her head and smiled, as if the question had been beside the point. "The past never quits following us around, does it?"

Before Sam could reply, a young man approached who had the looks of Travis in his youth. "Mama," said the young man, "it's time to go." He looked to Sam and smiled.

"Oh, I'm sorry," said Lora. "Sam, this is my youngest son. Carter, meet an old friend of your daddy, Sam Witherspoon."

Sam nodded approvingly at the young man's firm handshake. "Me and your daddy fought alongside each other over in the Nam."

Carter brightened at the comment and then said, "Sorry, Mr. Witherspoon, but we need to go." He led Lora off to a black limo.

By the time Sam turned into the pool hall parking lot, he had his tie off, his white shirt unbuttoned halfway down. He'd decided against making the trip to the cemetery. He figured he'd made a fool of himself with Lora; no telling now what she thought of him and his clumsy offer of a dinner date. Archie's car still sat in its usual spot, mirroring sunlight back to the west. No sign of customers, not even Donnie, his most faithful. He stood in the doorway for a moment, accustoming himself to the dim light.

"You ain't gonna guess who just left here, not five minutes ago," said Archie.

Sam rolled up his sleeves and began wiping down the already shiny bar.

"You ain't gonna guess?"

"Just tell me."

"Does the name Hueldine ring a bell?"

Sam dropped the cloth.

Archie squinted through the open rafters to the corrugated metal roof. "Hueldine Dizzer-sumpin," he said.

"Deshotels," said Sam. "Hueldine Deshotels."

Sam had managed to get over losing Lora to Travis after a while, and when his uncle died and left him the pool hall, he'd begun asking around for someone to see. An old friend from his high school days had moved to Montgomery and, during a chance meeting, the man directed Sam to the state's capitol city and to Hueldine. They'd gotten on well from the first date and, quickly pregnant, she'd agreed to marry Sam. Then she'd miscarried, during her third month. They went ahead with the marriage. For no particular reason, other than that they now lived in Montgomery, Sam had kept their union pretty much on the QT as far as Striven was concerned. Hueldine's father had been a chef for the Old Cloverdale Restaurant, once Montgomery's oldest and finest, and that had opened up new vistas for Sam. He'd worked there on Wednesday nights as a waiter, and in that role he'd met much of the city's old money crowd. But the marriage had

had the life of most impulsive liaisons; it had only lasted eighteen months, and Sam had moved back into his mobile home in Striven.

Archie waved an envelope.

"She sat down, right there at the bar," said Archie, "took a long time writing it."

Sam held out a hand for the torn-open envelope.

"She done that." Archie thumbed the frayed opening. "Don't worry, buddy, I didn't read it."

Sam smiled. Archie was what schoolteachers benevolently called a slow reader – he had dyslexia – he could hardly read beyond his own name. Sam pulled up a barstool. When he'd finished reading, he shoved the letter into a hip pocket.

Hueldine had been driving to Atlanta to visit her younger sister, had decided to detour to Striven and see if the old pool hall was still there. She'd written that she'd been shocked to discover Sam was still operating the place. He scowled. Then he pulled out the letter and re-read a particularly hurtful passage:

> *I always knew you had a hard time letting go of things, Sam, but I was really surprised that you've been hanging on to this old pool hall. I guess that was the problem between us, wasn't it? You just had to keep one foot in Montgomery and the other in Striven.*
>
> *I've wondered all these years whether you took Papa's lessons to heart – made of*

*yourself what you could've been. Anyway, I hope
you're happy with the choice you made.*

Sam frowned. *What did she expect? That I'd leave
Striven for good, maybe get some of her daddy's big-shot customers to
set me up for a run at the city council?* There had been silly talk
to that effect, but Sam couldn't've done it; his head was
still full of snakes from Vietnam. *Anyway*, he thought now,
I was never meant for such high cotton.

For the most part, Sam had become comfortable
with his solitary lot. It was only at times like this, during
the Christmas season, that he felt something missing. That
was when he fantasized about opening presents on
Christmas morning, big holiday meals with a wife and kids
and in-laws, and lately, having grandkids hanging from his
arms and legs as he watched TV at night. He turned the
letter over and once more read Hueldine's postscript.

*And in case you're wondering, Sam –
I never remarried. Never made the time for it, I
guess. First, looking after Daddy and the
restaurant, then my law degree and all that.
Guess some of us were never meant for marriage.*

I guess so, thought Sam. *Leastways, that's how it turned
out for us.* He re-folded the letter and pressed it back into
his pocket.

"She's a looker," said Archie. "That old flame still
burning?"

"Not hardly."

Well," said Archie, "If I was a betting man, I'd say she still carries a torch for you."

Sam looked up. He couldn't tell whether or not Archie was kidding. Or maybe he was just fishing for information he could shape into gossip.

"I'm closing up until after Christmas," Sam said.

Archie's face fell. "You ain't never done that before."

"You seen anybody in here this past week? Nobody's got a dime this Christmas. Anyway, it costs me to stay open."

Archie looked down, kicked at the dusty poolroom floor. "Okay, okay," he said, "you don't have to get all upset over it."

Sam snatched up a broom. "Go on, now. You got a family. Go spend some time with 'em."

Archie plodded toward the door, then stopped and turned. "Wilda said to ask you over for Christmas dinner."

Sam frowned. "I don't know."

Archie bowed his head to hide a smile. "She said you'd be like that. Said to keep on about it 'til you give in."

For years, Sam had made a practice of not accepting holiday invitations. He would've enjoyed the visits, to be sure, but it always made things back at his mobile home seem bleak. "I got stuff to do," he mumbled. "Get on home."

"I'll stop by," said Archie, "see if I can change your mind. Maybe we can play cards or sumpin."

Sam waved him out the door.

He made a few furious swipes at the floor with the broom. He hadn't read the paper that morning, so he set the broom aside, and for a while he stared blankly at his paper's pages. Then he resumed sweeping. He finished wiping down the bar and turned down the thermostat. He made sure the rear door was padlocked. Then he turned out the lights and left.

Archie did stop by the next day, and the next. They watched a bowl game on TV, played a few hands of rummy without keeping score. On Christmas Eve, Archie stopped by with a casserole Wilda had made.

"She said what with you being so hard-headed and all, she reckoned dinner would have to come to you." Archie handed Sam the dish.

No one had ever done this before. Sam's throat caught as he thanked Archie.

"It's just her string bean and mushroom soup dish," said Archie, "with some fried onions thowed in. Keep you from eating outta cans for a day or two." He stepped down from the mobile home's steps. "Merry Christmas, Sam."

Christmas dawned cold and hoary, but by midmorning the day had warmed. Sam thought about going bird hunting but decided not to; a shotgun booming on Christmas Day wasn't the sort of noise people nearby would want to hear. So he fed his chickens, gave his blue tick hound Luther a bath, set him on the deck out back to dry off, and made an egg sandwich to go with his coffee.

He decided late in the afternoon to call someone. It didn't matter who; it was just his way of having a moment of – what was it someone had called it? Communion. His way of having a manageable moment or two of conversation on the day everyone else was opening packages and getting ready for Christmas dinner. He had a cousin, Effie, in Missouri, already a widow and, like Sam, childless.

He dialed – no answer. Effie had been in poor health for a decade. He wondered if she'd died; there'd be no one to tell him if she had. Will it happen for me that way, too? No, he thought. Striven was his home, he'd known everyone there since he was a tot. Come to think of it, that was probably why people stayed in little towns, so somebody would notice if you died.

He flipped on the TV – a parade in New York City had just begun. Luther squeezed through the dog door, lapped up water from his bowl, leaped onto the sofa, and lay his head in Sam's lap. The phone rang.

"Sam, it's Lora."

He sat up straight, cleared his throat. "Lora?"

She laughed nervously. "Guess you're surprised that I'd call, especially on Christmas morning."

He grunted something along the lines of *uh huh*.

"Look, Sam, I'm so sorry we had such a hurried conversation. Was I terribly rude?"

"You had your mind on Travis," he said. "I reckon I was the rude one, wanting to get you off like that, start on about, well, what might've been." He swallowed, hard. "I'm mighty sorry I did that."

"Well, I'm not, Sam. Carter and Junior kept telling me all afternoon that I needed to put Travis to rest, you know, in my mind."

Sam said nothing as he scratched Luther's long ears.

"Sam?"

"Yeah, I'm here, Lora."

"Well, I was wondering if you'd like to come to Montgomery sometime, maybe in a month or so. We could have that dinner and catch up." A pause. "Or maybe I could cook dinner. The restaurants around here, they're all so noisy nowadays. It's hard to have a conversation."

Silence.

"Sam?'

"You're just full of s'prises, Lora."

"Then you'll call? In maybe a month?"

Sam frowned, slowly shook his head. "Maybe," he said.

A relieved laugh. "I'm looking forward to it, Sam."

Sam's frown remained for a minute or so after he hung up. Then he rose, peered into the refrigerator, sniffed the remains of Wilda's casserole, and spooned it into a bowl. He opened a beer and again flopped onto the couch. When he'd finished the casserole and beer, he clicked through TV channels and settled on a pregame football show. Luther rose on his forelegs, yawned, stretched, and set his head back on Sam's lap. Midway into the game's first quarter, Sam's chin settled onto his chest. His eyes fluttered and closed. Moments later, he was snoring.

CHAPTER VI

The door had creaked open, the rectangular gap sundered by Archie's gangly frame. He grinned at Donnie. "You bragging on your mama again, huh?"

Donnie didn't reply, so Archie, in his socially awkward way, looked to Sam. "I don't 'member much about your mama, Sam, but I bet she was smart as a whip, too."

Donnie picked up his cue, held it to the rafters and, rolling it with nimble fingers, sighted down its taper. Then he chalked up and stroked the cue ball. A pair of striped balls rattled toward the corner pockets. As they disappeared, he winked at Archie. Then he threw a glance Sam's way. "You the only one here," he said to Archie, "who's gonna have people around to sing your praises when you hit the dirt side of the sod."

Archie eyed them both and nodded. "That little daughter of mine, and them twins of hers, they'll be Johnny on the spot then, 'specially them two little ones. Don't know what I'd do without 'em. You two ever get lonesome for grandkids?"

Donnie leaned his stick against the table, fingered a smoke from his shirt pocket, and lit it. Another wink. "I got my Mama. Sam here ain't got squat, 'cept Lu, and it ain't for sure she's gonna stick around."

Sam bristled at that, picked up his paper, and sat. He shook a pair of pages apart.

"Hey Sam!" said Archie. "If Lu packs her bags on you, I know this cute little gal you could run off with."

"She ain't gotta be cute," said Donnie. "Ol' Sam can't see too good nohow."

"Pull yourself a beer off that tap," Sam said to Archie, "and y'all shut up."

Archie's chin quivered.

"He's been that way all morning," said Donnie. "Don't know what's come over him."

Archie blew out a long breath and then drawled, "I guess a fellow that runs a pool hall's liable to have a mood now and again."

THE RIGHT THING

The long, shotgun-style building swelled with the usual cheers of its pool shooters' triumphs, the accompanying groans of errant shots, and these all but drowned out the girlish laughter just outside the open front door to Sam's Place. Then a line of feminine figures passed through the entryway. The regulars' noise eddied to a hush.

Five girls had entered, or at least they seemed girls, college students, maybe, dressed in shorts and tees, split-sided skirts and halter-tops. But something about them – nothing you could put your finger on – seemed far removed from the silly, giggly ways of college girls on a weekend outing.

Donnie took a deep draw from his smoke and leered. "You girls looking for a little action, I bet."

One of the five turned a scornful stare on him. "I sure hope you mean pool action."

Donnie chuckled. "Well, sugar, we ain't got no swimming pool, but I reckon we can find one, if that's what it takes."

A spate of timorous male laughter fluttered about the five.

Donnie began to preen. He brushed at his yellowed shirtsleeves, flicked the back of a hand at a bit of ash on the front of his jeans, and finished with a nuanced crotch-grab. Then he gave his pals a grin and took another pull from his smoke.

"C'mon, girls," he said. "What you here for? We got a spare table over yonder by the bar. Y'all don't look like the bashful type, so drop them britches and let's go to it."

Sam lurched from his stool before the bar.

"Asshole," one of the women muttered.

Sam aimed a finger at Donnie. "You hush up, now," he said. He eyed the five, and then he glanced back to the snaggled-tooth shooter. "Donnie ain't never been able to back up that big mouth of his, so y'all don't pay him no mind."

Donnie blushed. A thread of smoke trailed from each nostril and curled over him like a pair of ibex horns.

"Uncouth primate," another of the women said.

Still another of the five, a short, black woman with an abundant figure, stepped forward. She poked Donnie's concave chest with a forefinger. "That the way you act around women, huh?" She turned to her friends. "What d'y'all think? I say we throw a bucket of whupass on this guy."

The woman's sass took Donnie aback for a moment. Then, as the women began to laugh, he sneered. "You think you can whup me, huh? You and what army?"

The woman, Joyce, gave him an ivory grin. "This army, I'd say." That brought another spate of laughter from her friends.

As Joyce and Donnie eyed one another, a sixth woman clomped up the front steps and into the pool hall.

She was as attractive as the others, despite the black athletic shoes, camouflage pants, and the black tee she wore, which had been emblazoned with a bone-white skull. A barbed wire tattoo peeked from below the right sleeve of her tee. Her purposeful stride across the room to her compatriots failed to disguise a limp.

"What's going on?" she asked. "These guys don't want us to play here?"

Joyce's stare remained on Donnie, who began to blink. He backed away a step.

"Looks that way," said Joyce.

Two of the women exchanged glances. One said, "They think we're hookers, Luann."

Donnie raised a palm in defense. "I was just funning a little bit, that's all."

"We get college girls in here like that once in a while," said Wilson, another regular. He scratched his bald head and grinned. "Don't reckon college boys' talleywhackers do much for them gals, so they come here for a dose of the real deal."

Joyce scowled as the men laughed. Then she jabbed a finger at Wilson's belly orb and drew back a slapping hand. Donnie dropped his smoke, bounded up to her, and began his version of a boxer's bob and weave.

"All right!" said Luann. She stepped between Joyce and the two men. "At ease, everyone!"

Archie, Sam's most dependable regular, frowned down on the group of women from his six-and-a-half-feet of height. "You ladies sure are acting tough. A fella'd think you'd just got back from I-raq or sumpin."

"They haven't been there yet," Luann said. She tapped her chest. "But I have."

Snickers from Sam's regulars.

"You think I'm kidding?" She interlocked both hands under one knee and lifted her foot to the nearest pool table. Then she hiked up her pant leg to expose a thin, metallic shaft where her leg should've been.

The tittering trailed away. Sam's regulars edged up for a closer look.

A wry grin from Luann. "That's right, have a look – a good look. The highest-tech prosthesis the U.S. Army has."

Wilson edged ahead of Donnie and eyed Luann. "You really been to I-raq?"

"Fallujah," said Luann. "That's where I lost my leg."

"Hell you say," said Archie.

"In oh-four." Luann set her jaw, eyes narrowed.

"I remember seeing sumpin 'bout that on TV," Archie said.

Luann pinched her lips together and gave him a who-cares shrug. Then her brow furrowed, as if trying to make a tough decision. "The Marines," she began, slowly, "were a few bodies short. So our Airborne and the British Black Watch volunteered to help out." She sniffed and, speaking more rapidly now, she continued. "The jarheads wanted to keep us out of it – they'd been having a blood feud with the locals. But we said we'd come to fight, so they finally said come on. We grouped on the south side of the city that day, behind a wedge of Abrams tanks.

About daylight, the Abrams began laying down some serious suppressive fire." Luann stopped and glanced from face to face. "Any of you fellows serve in Vietnam?"

A couple of hands went up.

"Well," she said, "it was going to be a replay of the battle of Hue. Ever hear about that, up near North Vietnam? We were going to have to dig out Al-Zarqawi's fighters house by house, just like they did with the Viet Cong in Hue City."

Sam's regulars bent forward. The fan sitting in the building's gable sent its blades circling with oscillating whispers.

"So the tanks move on in," Luann went on. "A group of Seabees with 'dozers start pushing debris out of our way. The Marines go first, then the Brits, then us.

"We have to move slow, because the Air Force and Navy are bombing and strafing the streets. They even put a little white phosphorus on the populace. As we move in, we pass bodies with big chemical burns, some right through their skulls, others with the meat chewed off their arms and legs, right down to the bones. Pretty soon, Al-Zarqawi's people start fighting back, and let me tell you, those guys can fight.

"Counterattacks pop up everywhere: snipers on the rooftops, kids with Kalashnikovs, women with grenade launchers, the whole nine yards. Pretty soon, my team gets caught in a crossfire between three snipers. Deadly as hell when you don't have spotters or helo support. One of the snipers takes out our radio operator.

The bullet plows into his armpit and somehow ends up in the radio on his back.

"Then Willis, our platoon leader, he notices a big shell of a building up ahead, just beyond an overturned bus. He motions, tells us we're gonna set up in it.

"'Willis,' I yell, 'don't you see those fools behind that bus? There must be a dozen peeking over it. It's a trap!'

"He looks again and says, 'You, Shea, and Moncrief get a couple of clips ready. I'll keep Whittaker and Ali with me. Whittaker can lay out a line of grenades from the bus to the building. I'll keep the snipers busy.'

"So I take a deep breath, reload, huddle with Shea and Moncrief for a minute. Then off we go, Shea first, then me, and Moncrief last. It goes pretty well for the first couple of seconds, then Shea gets too close to one of Whittaker's grenade rounds. It takes off an arm and half a leg. Moncrief's on top of me by then. I decide to take a minute and tourniquet Shea's stumps. Then I hit him with a dose of morphine, pop in another clip, and Moncrief and I take off, side by side.

"The clowns behind the bus are firing, kicking up dust. Chips of rock and brick are hitting us, but they can't shoot as well as a bunch of Boy Scouts. I dive into the building, and that's when I hear Moncrief groan. A second later, he stumbles in, gut-shot. The round got in below his Kevlar."

Luann rocked back and forth, leaned onto her good leg. "Okay, so the plan is, once we're in the building, we're supposed to try and take out the guys behind the bus, then suppress the snipers while Willis, Whittaker, and Ali haul ass our way. I take a quick look at Moncrief. He's not too bad off, so I compress the wound and put on a bandage.

"'Can you fight?' I ask him. Moncrief says 'Hell, yeah.' So I get him positioned behind a pile of bricks so he can work on the guys at the bus. Then I give Willis a thumbs up, and I start taking potshots at the snipers.

"The crazy thing is, Willis and the other two take off, and one of the snipers stands up. I put one into his kaffiyeh, and he drops –" Luann eyed Donnie, and a flicker of mischief raced across her face, "– like a used rubber."

"Potty mouth," Donnie said, grinning. "I knowed you was my kind of gal."

Luann went on. "Then another one stands up, so he can see me, I guess. I put one into his shooting shoulder. The third one rises to a crouch, then drops and crawls away.

"Meanwhile, I guess Moncrief's pissed about being shot, because he starts putting a stream of rounds into the crowd at the bus, at least enough to keep 'em down until Willis, Whittaker, and Ali get to us. But on the way, Willis decides to stop by Shea for a second. Shea isn't moving.

"When Willis reaches me, he shouts, 'Your tie-offs didn't hold, he bled out.' I'm silent while Willis scratches his chin. Then he looks at me, and I'm crying. 'It ain't your fault, Adams,' he says. 'You did what you could for him, considering the circumstances.' That's when the old man starts jabbering."

At this point of the story, Joyce nodded, elbowed the woman next to her.

"You've heard this?" the other woman asked.

"Just once," said Joyce.

While Luann was spinning her tale, Sam had edged away and now stood alone, a deep frown pinching his face. Luann bit her lip, as if trying to stanch a crying spell. Sam's face relaxed into a sympathetic look. He retreated to the bar, drew a beer from the tap, returned, and handed it to Luann.

"You look like you need to wet your whistle," he said.

She studied him for a moment, took the plastic cup, and drank half.

"The old man?" asked Archie. "What old man?"

"Some old Iraqi," said Luann. "He's behind us with a half-dozen women and maybe eight or ten little kids." She held a hand out waist-high. "Not a one of those kids is over ten years old."

"You were lucky," said Joyce. "They could've been bad guys just as easy."

Luann looked to her shoes for a moment. "Then Ali – he's one of the Iraqi Army guys translating for us – he gets to jabbering at this bunch. They want food and water. Willis says it's okay, so we give 'em our MREs and a couple bottles of water. They eat like they're half starved.

"So a few minutes go by and they're eating – there's this lull in the fighting – and another platoon shows up on the opposite end of the street. A team of Brits. They take out the ones behind the bus, trot over, and let Willis use their radio. He calls a chopper, because Moncrief's leaking pretty bad by then, and Whittaker's been winged on the run across.

"We take a minute to put Shea in a bag. A few more minutes go by, and a couple of *Apache* gunships come in to clear the street. A MEDEVAC helo drops onto the rooftop next to us while the *Apaches* hover.

"'Adams,' Willis says to me, 'can you get Moncrief up those back steps?' 'I can,' I tell him, 'but I'm not leaving until these civilians are safe.' 'Safe?' he says, 'this is by-God Fallujah, Adams! Who the hell's safe around here?' I tell him, 'That's the way it's gonna be, Sarge. Get 'em out of the city, then the chopper can come get me.'

"Willis kicks up a cloud of dust and mutters something I won't repeat about women on the battlefield. Then Whittaker pipes up and says, 'I'll stay with her.' 'You're wounded, for chrissake,' says Willis. Whittaker just grins. 'I ain't bleeding right now,' he says. 'I'm gonna stay.'

"Meanwhile, Ali's herding the women and kids out and up the steps to the MEDEVAC. Willis carries Shea. Whittaker helps Moncrief, and a few minutes later he comes back, tells me there's no more room on the chopper. 'Sarge is really pissed,' he says. 'He's gonna Article Fifteen you when you get back.' 'He can court-martial me, for all I care,' I tell him. He sort of snickers, and that's that. We stay.

"It gets dark in an hour or so, and I start second guessing myself, thinking I should've gone, left the civilians to fend for themselves. We hear that Arab jibber-jabber through the night, knowing the bad guys are doing something out on the street. Our only hope is they won't have any idea Whittaker and I are in that old building.

"Well, the sun comes up hot and heavy, a film of smoke lying over the street, blue as one of those Persian rugs. But good old Willis – he has a rescue helo and three *Apaches* out at daybreak. The rescue chopper lands on the roof next door, and I hear Willis calling.

"'C'mon,' I say to Whittaker, 'let's get the hell outta Dodge.' He wants me to go first, but I say no, I'll cover you. He looks at me as if to say you idiot, and then he limps off. Nobody fires back, so I take off, running a little different path, in case snipers are already setting up shop. That's when this happens."

Luann bit her lip, face torqued with emotion. Then she reached down and rapped on the metal leg.

"You got shot?" asked Donnie.

"An improvised explosive device," said Luann. She took a deep breath. "I vaguely remember being airlifted out. Then I'm in a medical tent, and a surgeon's talking to me. Next thing I know, I'm in Ramstein, in Germany."

"Shitfire," said Donnie.

"I'll say," Archie added.

"Okay," said Luann, "that's my story. Now do my girls have the right to shoot a few games here without being hassled?"

"I always wanted to be in a fight like that," said Donnie.

Luann glanced his way, hawked, and spat at his feet.

Sam broke the silence. "Y'all can play all weekend if you want to. Won't cost you a dime." He looked to Luann. "How about another beer?"

"Got anything stronger?"

Sam smiled. "Got some Johnnie Walker. Be glad to share."

Luann returned the smile. Sam scrabbled around for a couple of shot glasses, wiped them with his bar rag, and poured. He skirted the bar and pulled up a couple of barstools. They drank for a while without speaking, the women hooting as they took turns shooting nine ball.

Luann glanced up to Sam, who was taking her in and beaming. "What?"

"Nothing," said Sam. "Not a thing."

"I don't think so," she said. "Why're you looking at me that way?"

He turned to his empty glass and poured more for both. "That story."

Luann eyed him and took a sip.

"You really shoot that good? I didn't figure you for a combatant."

She grinned and nodded. "Just came natural that day."

Sam waited for her to say more.

"I'm a medic," she went on. "I'm training these gals at Fort Rucker. When their class graduates, my service time'll be over and I'm retiring. Anyway, everyone in a firefight's a combatant. I just figured I'd better give your guys the Hollywood version, even if I didn't style myself exactly right. Damned if I was going to let them run all over us just because we're women."

Sam nodded slowly. "Only thing is, I don't know how you can make it through a story like that. I've never been able to tell some of my Nam tales without my brain getting out of joint."

"I'm just trying to get past it," she said. "Sometimes telling it helps." She nodded toward the other five. "Maybe hearing it'll help them when they get over there."

"Bad thing, though, losing a leg."

Luann's head hung and her shoulders slouched. "That's not it," she said. "I left Shea to die." She started a soft sobbing.

Sam patted her arm, then put his own across her shoulders and pulled her to him. "Maybe you coulda done more for him, and maybe you couldn't. But you done something a whole lot better."

She wiped her eyes. "The civilians?"

"It wasn't their war, Luann."

She sniffed and took another sip. "But did that make it right? I mean, does saving their lives make up for Shea?"

Another pat. "Don't try to figure it out," he said. "Just let it go."

She pushed away, rubbed her face dry, and they turned to watch the women shoot pool. The regulars were playing their own games, occasionally casting respectful glances at Luann.

The sun had angled so that its light began to stream through the louvered vents in the roof's build-out, where the fan sat. The fan blades sliced at the sunbeams, sending alternating shards of darkness and light over the shooters. After a while, Sam took Luann's hand. She used her metal leg to scoot her stool a fraction closer.

For some reason Sam hadn't been able to fathom, an uneasiness had been growing since mid-summer, when the longer shadows and vivid colors of fall had begun their slow formation. It was something he hadn't felt since his return from Vietnam. But now, as Luann snuggled into him, he hardly noticed it.

CHAPTER VII

Noxanne and Wilson, toothpicks hanging from their lips following breakfast at an all-you-can-eat Denny's in Auburn, had just clomped in. They snickered and elbowed one another.

"Sam don't have a mood once in a while," said Noxanne, "he comes to it as regular as I do my monthly."

"He's acting like he's done crawled in a hole and pulled the dirt in over hisself," said Donnie.

"What brought all this on?" asked Wilson.

Donnie eyed Sam. "Well, first off, he got a good grouch going about Brother Wilding. Claims the reverend's done him dirty somehow."

Wilson tossed his toothpick over his shoulder. "It was Wayman Tucker who did that. He tried to shut Sam's Place down a half dozen times."

"Then it ain't got nothing to do with Brother Wilding," said Donnie.

"Yeah it does, too," said Noxanne. "Him and Tucker's so close they might as well kiss."

An aha moment took Archie. "I guess I ain't surprised at that. I forgot about our good ol' chief of police and Wilding being cousins, sumpin like two, three times removed on Wayman's daddy's side."

Donnie glanced to the establishment's rear, where Sam was drawing a round of beers. An old memory had surfaced, a story Sam

99

had told only once, during an all-night drinking session, a night when Sam had been as snockered as anyone could remember. "Hey, Sam," he called out, chuckling. "'Member that gal you hooked up with over in Montgomery? Didn't you get her knocked up or some such?"

"I ain't had a kid with nobody," Sam said, eyes narrowed. "Leastwise, none I know of." He jabbed a finger at the line of foaming cups. "Y'all have a beer and lock up all the chitchat about something you don't know a damn thing about."

THE DAY THE BEER CAME

Donnie forced a thread of smoke through the gap in his front teeth, crushed out the butt in a sand-filled bucket and, scowling, he kicked the barstool Sam had set a water dispenser on. The ceramic water crock pitched left and right.

Sam eyed the crock, wiped a glaze of sweat from his brow with a chamois he'd bought that morning, and continued waxing the bar to a deep gleam.

Donnie lit another smoke. He cupped both hands on the crock. "This thing ain't worth the trouble it'd take to shoot a hole in it. Hot as a five dollar pistol."

Sam shambled the length of his bar, opened a freezer, and lifted out a small bag of crushed ice. "This is the last of it," he said.

Donnie pulled the plastic bag apart and dumped its dripping shards into the crock. Then he shook the crock and stuck a paper cup under its tap. He took a sip and then spat it against the unpainted plank wall. "Still hot." He turned a beseeching look to Sam. "Sure could use some ice cold beer."

The window air conditioner behind the bar at Sam's Place's was barely wheezing out enough refrigeration to keep the pool hall's temperature tolerable. But after all, it *was* early September, and this *was* Alabama.

101

Ice. Cold. Beer. Just thinking those words had to be torture to Sam's customers.

Normally he did a good business selling beer during summer's dog days. But that relief was temporarily adrift. The beer trucks had been passing his establishment by in recent weeks. His business was rural and small, the distributors kept reminding him during his ongoing phone calls. I'm afraid you're not a top priority, good buddy. You'll have to wait until we've taken care of the big-volume customers.

But Sam's regulars were becoming edgy amid the lack of icy adult beverages. He thought for a moment about the big knife fight of last fall and the trouble it had brought him; the last thing he needed was a houseful of pool shooters with short fuses. He came around the bar and shook the crock himself. Donnie was right. It was absorbing too much heat; the ice would melt before the water could turn cold enough to slake thirst. Good thing he had a back-up plan.

"Noxanne's got a double-walled water can," he said, "and she's gonna donate it for the rest of the summer."

Donnie eyed the crock. "Still don't see why you can't chill a few brews in that thing."

Sam was about to reply for the umpteenth time that bottled beer cost too much to keep on hand – and besides, the couple of cases he could afford would be gone in thirty minutes' time – when the front door opened. Wilson, until recently a regular, tottered at the threshold under the weight of girlfriend Noxanne's gigantic water can.

"Where you want this thing?" he asked, a line of sweat arcing down his pudgy face.

Donnie pulled the crock off the stool, clumped it to the floor, and slapped the stool's seat. Wilson nudged the water can onto it and stood back, evaluating the rickety barstool.

"Hope you brought ice like I asked," said Sam.

"Noxanne put it in the car," said Wilson. He glanced toward the door. "Might need some help with it, though. She's a little bit under the weather today. Don't think she can carry much."

"You tell her to get her fat ass in here," said a cranky Donnie. "We got lotsa thirsty people."

Wilson's eyes narrowed and his cheeks puffed. He normally took the aspersions and lewd comments about his girlfriend in stride, but lately he'd grown testy where Noxanne's checkered past was concerned. He sniffed, gave his nose a pugilist's thumb-brush. "If I was a lesser man, I'd make you eat them words."

Donnie smirked. "You mean if you was more of a man."

Wilson glared, took a step toward Donnie.

"The heat's got him," tall, sinewy Archie said to Wilson. "Don't pay him no mind." He put an arm across Wilson's sweaty shoulders. "Why come you being so testy?"

Donnie grinned and bounced on his toes. "Ol' Wilson's been that way since he moved in with Noxanne."

He poked Wilson's potbelly. "Shacking up's not agreeing with y'all, that it? You can't live on love, huh?"

Wilson pursed his lips and didn't answer.

"Where is the old gal, anyway?" Donnie asked. "I ain't seen her in a month of Sundays." Another poke to Wilson's belly. "Bet she don't want to be seen much. I 'member last time she was in here she looked like she was putting on a ton of weight."

Wilson raised a finger, shook it.

Just then, Noxanne stepped into the doorway wearing a gaudy Hawaiian muumuu instead of her usual tee shirt and cutoff jeans. She staggered, dropped the bag of ice she'd been carrying, and clutched her belly. Wilson hurried to her. He set a hand on her egg-shaped abdomen, and then touched his cheek to hers. "What is it, sugar?"

She grunted, as if in the throes of a bowel movement. "Hurts."

Wilson looked to Sam. "I think we gonna need Doc Quincey."

"What's wrong with her?" Sam asked.

Wilson's brow furrowed. "Might be her 'pendix."

Sam dialed, spoke a few words, and hung up. "Doc ain't in town. He's gone fishing for a couple of days."

"Oh, Lord!" said Noxanne. She slumped to a sitting position on the plank floor, hiked the muumuu above her knees, legs spread. "Oh, Lord! Lord have mercy!"

As Noxanne's wailing rose above the men's chatter, Sam's front door edged open. A broad-backed woman began bumping quietly up the steps with a set of hand trucks. She dragged her burden across the threshold and turned the shiny, new fifteen-gallon beer keg on its end before her. Mesmerized by Noxanne's screaming, no one noticed her.

"Air!" yelled Wilson, who had dropped to all fours beside Noxanne. "We need to breathe some down here. Y'all move back!" He pulled a wrinkled handkerchief from a hip pocket and wiped Noxanne's face and neck.

The other men backed a step away – except Donnie, who edged forward. He squinted, evaluating Noxanne. "She got the trots or sumpin? She ain't been putting prune juice in her whiskey again, has she?"

Wilson looked up, his expression raw with concern. "I tole you, her 'pendix might bust. We gotta get her to that hospital over in Montgomery. Can somebody drive us over there in Noxanne's van?"

Archie stepped up, bent over the agonized couple. "Y'know, I seen this before, and it ain't no 'pendix."

"Is too!" said Wilson. "I done figured it out."

"Oh, mama!" yelled Noxanne. "I'm gonna explode!"

"It ain't no 'pendix," Archie repeated. "This gal's about to pop out a young'un. I seen it when my own was born."

Sam's jaw dropped. He leaned across the bar. "She's pregnant?"

Wilson's head dropped, eyes to the floor. "Yeah."

"Oh, Jesus Lord in heaven," said Noxanne. She slid prone. "Damn your pecker, Wilson Noonsocket!" Her body quivered as if she'd grabbed a live wire and couldn't let go. "Get this devil outta me!"

"It ain't no devil, honey pie," said Wilson. He lifted a sodden clump of hair from her face. "It's ours, just like I been saying. It's ours."

The woman who had entered with the beer keg, still unnoticed by the crowd, reached into a hip pocket, fished out a pack of cigarettes, and lit a smoke. She frowned as she expelled a long, white stream.

Another wave of tremors passed through Noxanne. She pulled her knees up, legs wide.

"Holy mackerel!" said one of the on-looking men. "Look at that."

Donnie bent sideways and peered. Then he swallowed, Adam's apple bobbing. He turned away and gagged.

Wilson glared at the men. "All right, y'all stop that gawking, stop it right now! She don't like to wear underpants, that's all."

"She's split wide open," Donnie replied. "Looks like somebody hit her with a pole axe." He glanced about, as if looking for a place to throw up, then shook his head and swallowed. He took a long draw from his cigarette.

"They call that dilating," said Archie.

"I got some towels behind the bar," said Sam.

"What the hell we gonna do with towels?" said Donnie, his Adam's apple pulsing.

Sam shook his head. "I heard you need some, that's all."

"Awright, then," said Archie, waggling a hand at Sam. "She's gonna need hot water, too. Can you heat some water?"

"Got a hot plate," said Sam.

"You son of a bitch!" squalled Noxanne. "Get this bastard outta me!"

"O, Jesus, Jesus," said Wilson. "What we gonna do?"

Sam filled a saucepan with water, clattered it onto the hot plate. "It's gonna be a few minutes. This thing don't heat up all that fast."

The beer woman took a long draw from her smoke and huffed at all this. She opened her mouth to speak just as Noxanne renewed her screaming. Wilson joined in with his own howls. Noxanne grabbed Wilson's wrist and squeezed, hard. The beer woman clamped her jaw shut and watched silently.

"Let go, girl," said Wilson. "I'm right here."

She emitted a low, guttural sound and turned loose. Another spasm. Her face reddened. More screaming and cursing.

"It was back the first of January, when the power went out all over town," Wilson said. "That's when she got pregnant."

"Don't imagine she took it well, knowing her," said Sam.

"She cussed a blue streak when she quit having her monthly." Wilson rubbed his wrist. "We went to one of them clinics last month, but they said she was into her third semester, and they couldn't do the procedure."

107

"*Tri*mester, I think it's called," said Archie. "Not *se*mester."

Wilson glanced to the moaning Noxanne. "Time just caught up with us."

Donnie bent low, peered into the shadows of Noxanne's skirt, toward the confluence of her cellulite-faceted legs. His Adam's apple bobbed again. "Damn, that's an ugly sight."

Noxanne blinked. "You…didn't think so…back…when we –"

"Hush," said Wilson, "I don't want to hear stuff like that."

Noxanne wiped a string of drool from her lips. "You didn't think…you was getting…a virgin…"

"Hush, girl," said Wilson.

Then a wave of fluid gushed from between Noxanne's legs. Simultaneously, Donnie and Archie stepped back.

"Holy moly!" said Donnie.

Archie nodded. "Yep, one's about to bust on out."

Donnie pointed. "What the hell is that?"

"That's the top of its head," said Archie.

Donnie gurgled, pitched his smoke across the room, lunged for the sand bucket beside the water can, and puked. Then fresh screams from Noxanne.

Sam came around the bar and stepped into the midst of the retching and howling with a saucepan full of water and a pair of ragged towels. He looked to Archie. "What you want to do with these?"

Archie blinked. "*Me?* I don't know nothing about delivering babies."

Donnie wiped a shirtsleeve across his mouth, licked his lips. "Sure could use a beer." He glanced toward the door. "Hot awmighty," he said, "the beer's here!"

With that, everyone turned. They cheered.

The woman glared at Donnie and said, "Looking at a woman's privates and then throwing up. You're an absolute skunk." She hitched at her jeans, brushed them flat, and then tugged at the under-sized football jersey she wore. The jersey had been lopped at the shoulders, revealing a pair of dragon tattoos winding down her muscular arms. She stuck her cigarette into one corner of her mouth, squinted, and extended a hand to Archie. "Here," she said, "give me those towels. And stand ready with that water." She ran a hand across her flattop and knelt at Noxanne's feet.

"You know how to do this?" Archie asked.

The woman nodded. "I was an EMT until last year." She put out her cigarette on the heel of one boot and took the towels.

"You ain't now, though," said Sam, as if a question.

She glanced up and cleared her throat. "They let me go."

"Sorry to hear it," said Sam.

"It was a personal thing."

Noxanne tore into a new set of tremors and screams and curses.

The woman put her hand on Noxanne's abdomen, gently pushed Noxanne's legs apart with her knees, and folded the muumuu back. "My name's Connie, sweetheart," the woman said over Noxanne's bellowing. "I want you to breathe, deep."

With difficulty, Noxanne did.

"When you feel a contraction, I want you to push."

Moments later, a tiny head came fully into view.

"The little sumbitch is blue," said Donnie.

Another push from Noxanne, and more cursing.

"Got sumpin around its neck," said Archie.

"Umbilical cord," said Connie. "That's why the face turned blue. Not getting enough air." She reached into a pocket, pulled out a large pocketknife, dipped it in the water, and parted the cord in two places. She carefully unwound the umbilical piece, removed it and set it on the floor.

Another set of contractions pushed the baby free – a chubby, red-faced girl.

"I need a wrap for her," Connie said.

Archie volunteered an old sweatshirt from the trunk of his car. She had him slit it at one side and cut off the sleeves. Then she wrapped the baby in the makeshift blanket. She rose and was about to hand the girl to Wilson when Noxanne kicked Connie's foot.

"Give her to me."

Wilson took the baby. "I ain't gonna, sugar. You said you didn't want no baby, said it was all a big mistake, your biggest one ever." He looked around. "You all heard her, she called this baby a devil, cussed like a sailor while she was having it." He turned to his prostrate lover. "It's my baby, too, you know, and I don't want you hurting her." Then he looked down, smiled, and touched the baby's tiny nose. "I always did want a little girl."

Noxanne groaned as she forced herself to a sitting position against someone's legs. "Wilson, you gimme that baby."

Connie nudged Wilson. "It'll be all right. The crying, the swearing, it's all part of the birthing experience."

Wilson knelt and settled the baby onto Noxanne's breast.

Noxanne curled her chubby arms around the tiny figure. She smiled. Then she kissed the baby's cheeks. She rocked the infant back and forth and began a soft, out-of-tune song.

"Who'd a thunk that?" said Donnie. "She's acting like a real mama." He turned to Wilson. "What's its name?"

"It ain't no it," said Wilson. "It's a she. And we ain't decided."

"Both of them need washing," said Connie, wiping her hands on one of Sam's towels. "And someone needs to clean up the afterbirth."

"You do it," Donnie said.

Connie gave him a look.

Archie whistled out a breath. "I'll do it. I got a box of rags in my car." He returned from his car moments later with a cardboard box full of mechanic's cloths.

Wilson took the baby. With one hand, he helped Noxanne up. Then he led the groaning mother out the door.

Archie cleaned up and carried the bloody mass to the trash barrel out back. Connie trucked the keg down the aisle between the pool tables and to the pool hall's rear. Sam hooked up the keg and bled off the foam.

"I got dibs on the first pull off that keg," said Donnie. "That fuss made me thirstier'n I was already."

Archie returned, clouded with the smell of kerosene and smoke.

"Archie gets the first pull," said Sam. "He did the cleaning up."

Archie shook his head. "Give it to Connie here. She pulled our bacon outta the fire."

At first Connie didn't respond. Then she sighed and waggled a hand for the beer.

Sam drew a cupful and handed it across the bar.

"Speech!" someone yelled.

"Yeah," said Archie. "You the lady of the hour."

Connie took a long drink and then eyed the men. "I would've never believed you guys could be as ignorant of women as you are."

Silence.

"Ma'am," said Donnie. "This ain't part of what we know —"

Connie huffed. "Your friend Wilson knew enough to get her pregnant."

Donnie grinned. "Well, that part comes natural."

A titter of laughter.

Connie extracted her cigarette pack from the rear pocket, discovered it was empty. She reached into Donnie's shirt pocket and pulled a smoke from his pack. She eyed him, as if to say, "Well?"

He fished out a lighter and lit it for her.

Connie followed her first stream of smoke as it writhed its way toward the building's rafters. "Except for the fact that everything worked out," she said, "I'd be tempted to line you boneheads up and slap each of you into next week."

"Say what?" said Donnie.

"Dumbasses," said Archie. "She just called us dumbasses."

"You boys are pitiful," said Connie. "Today a woman helped another woman bring a little girl into the world, and all you could do was stand there and gawk."

While she drank her beer, the pool hall denizens remained silent. Then she ripped a bill from a pad, handed it to Sam, and headed out the door.

No one spoke until the beer truck had disappeared.

Archie peered out the door to the truck's dust. Then he turned to the others and shook his head. "That old gal's a real piece of work."

Donnie frowned and shook his head. "Don't think I'll ever understand women, even if I live to be a hundred."

CHAPTER VIII

Archie and Wilson looked to their shoes. They hadn't heard about the Reverend Wesley Wilding being so directly involved in trying to shut down Sam's, and that was surprising in a gossipy little town like Striven. Too, Archie and Wilson knew better than to ask Sam more about it; experience had taught them that you just shouldn't pry into certain areas of Sam's life.

Donnie, though, was undeterred. "You 'member, Sam, we was up to our ears in corn liquor one night, and —"

Sam's glare deepened. "Drop it, I said."

Donnie pushed with both hands at the air between Sam and him. "Okay, okay, don't get yourself all worked up, now. I just thought…"

Noxanne put a hand on Donnie's arm and peered to the bar. "You say them beers is for us?"

"Yeah," said Sam, "if y'all can see fit to shut up about my private doings."

Wilson, afraid Sam's temper still might boil over, changed the subject. "Funny things happen when you get off the battlefield, huh, Sam?"

A quizzical look. "I reckon."

"What I mean is, you could of took a job, any job a'tall, over in Montgomery after that discharge of yours."

For a moment, Sam said nothing. Then he sighed through a now-saddened expression. "They wasn't all that fond of soldiers back then. *Some of us got turned down for jobs <u>because</u> we was ex-soldiers."*

"I 'member hearing 'bout when you got out," said Donnie. "You took a job sweeping up this place for your Uncle Clifton. Didn't make much sense, even to a kid like me."

"You ever been to a war, you'd know," said Sam, "'specially one that was lost." He whistled out a breath, his eyes fixed on some faraway thing. "Damn war stayed with me for quite a spell. Sweeping up helped keep me outta the doldrums."

THE OUTER MASQUERADE

"Well," said a grinning Donnie, "looky who's back in town, and looking fit as a pair of dang fiddles, too."

With that, a clamor of greetings rose from the regulars at Sam's Place.

Slim, the old pool shark, returned the grin and patted his young sidekick Tommy's back. "We was passing through, y'see? Tommy said it'd be a crime if we didn't stop in and say howdy."

Tommy had frequented Sam's pool hall in earlier seasons. Although he was still a few chin hairs short of adulthood, the crest of his barely controlled cowlick reached more than six feet above the dusty floor, and a wispy blond mustache seemed in accord with his sparse sideburns. A new black jacket and turtleneck shirt clung to his narrow shoulders. Below the legs of his pipestem jeans, a pair of black boots peeked out, reflecting the light cast by the closest pool table's fluorescent fixture. He winked at the crowd and whispered to the old man. Other than age, they seemed about as alike as two peas born of the same pod.

Sam looked up from his bar sink. Had it really been almost two years since he and Slim had conspired to hustle Tommy in order to break him of his pool shooting dreams? The kid's widowed mama had told Sam later on that Tommy had hardly slept the night Slim skinned him out of his only ten-dollar bill. The boy got up bleary-eyed and morose the next morning and, after an hour of TV news and three cups of strong coffee, he stumbled off for work at Striven's only grocery store.

But he never showed up for work. He'd dipped surreptitiously into his mama's money before leaving home and, after asking questions around town about Slim's whereabouts, he struck out hitchhiking towards Montgomery. When Sam heard that, he knew: Tommy was following Slim. The boy would likely throw down the gauntlet again, and Slim would beat him again. Then he'd slink back to Striven and the humdrum that swallows the rural towns of central Alabama.

That wasn't the way it happened, though. As a pool shooter, Tommy had always grown at a gallop and, so the stories went that floated back to Sam, he started taking on all comers, from Montgomery to San Antonio. Finally, he called Slim out in a dimly lit pool hall in Port Arthur, down near the Texas coast. He took the old man; beat him out of three hundred dollars, most of Slim's ready cash.

Undaunted and always with an eye out for a new hustle, Slim teamed up with the boy and pushed him on unsuspecting two-bit hustlers around the South. Finally, word got out about the kid, and Slim had to stop using the boy that way. After that, the drifters' grapevine had proclaimed Slim and Tommy's partnership one of equals.

Sam was about to call out and inquire into the pair's latest doings when Archie, the house's lankiest shooter, bent across his table to better take in the two hustlers and their new clothes, and said, "The game paying *that* good out yonder?"

Slim lifted a skeletal hand to his mouth and quietly coughed into it. "I been showing Tommy the ropes." He wiped at a bit of what seemed in the dim light to be snuff drool. Then he grinned. "He's getting so good I got to run to keep up, though."

"We're partners," said Tommy. He put a hand on Slim's shoulder and gave those ancient bones a comradely shake. "We incorporated last month."

"Hell you say," said Archie. "What for?"

"Pool's a paying sport now," said Tommy. "We even got us a sponsor. *Sticktec* wanted us, gave us a three-year exclusive." He nodded. "We're big-time."

Sam had just finished washing out a dozen shot glasses and was wiping them dry. A glass in hand, he stepped around the bar and shuffled toward the pair. He'd never been big on Tommy, despite the boy's talent, and he found himself frowning at the smug pronouncement. "What brought this on?" he asked of Slim. "Thought you was gonna stay free-lance 'til the day you die."

Slim's eyes flicked toward the boy. His mouth drew to a wary line. "Tommy's been reading up on things. He got one of them laptops, follers the sport news, the bidness end of the game."

Still twisting a tongue of cloth inside the shot glass, Sam looked back and forth between the two. Pool shooting had gone corporate years earlier, abetted by the Newman film and Newman's pairing with the boy with the toothy grin. What was his name? Anyway, it was all about money. The color of it.

But Slim had scoffed at such endorsements for years. He was old school to a fault; he'd always stuck to the backwoods and inner city pool halls, going with his gut and his mouth to make what living he could with the breakdown pool cue he protected like a teen-aged daughter's virtue. He'd show up in Vegas or Chicago in those faded, paper-thin clothes of his, and with an equally flimsy bankroll. As the seedy-looking shooter walked among the tournament tables, a titter of derisive laughter would snake through them. Slim never cared, though. In fact, if half the stories making their way back to Striven could be taken at face value, Slim's scruffiness and cocksure persona were pretty much why other shooters tended to underestimate his talents. But then they usually ended up a couple of C-notes lighter in the wallet. So, Sam wondered, what had caused Slim to change his tune?

Slim opened his jacket wide, displaying the Neiman-Marcus label stitched on the inside pocket. He did a clumsy model's turn with the jacket flared, looking for all the world like a loopy angel with wings akimbo. He let the jacket fall back into place. Squinting, he brushed with painstaking precision at a few motes of lint on the sleeves.

Then he looked up and, noting Sam's frown, he cleared his throat. "Now don't go thinking we're getting uppity. These glad rags of ours was our agent's idea. We got to have the right kind of image for *Sticktec.*"

No one said a word. Someone cleared his throat in a contemptuous manner, and the pool hall began to fill with the scrapes of shuffling shoes as Sam's shooters drifted back to their tables and a new round of racks.

"That's right nice, and all," said Sam, "but I'm having a hard time seeing you as a mouthpiece for a bunch like that."

Tommy stepped into the space between the two older men. "It ain't really about pool shooting no more, Mister Sam. It's about the numbers."

Sam's sour expression deepened.

"Y'see," said Tommy, "it don't really matter how good you are with a stick. Well, it does, but you gotta get ink in the right publications, so the companies'll know who you are. Once you get a couple of endorsements, the agents come calling." He gave Slim a sidelong glance plump with pride. "A good agent'll land the fans for you. And that's money in the bank."

Sam cocked his head to one side and looked to Slim. The old pool shark nodded, but his agreement seemed more acquiescence than zeal. Sam shook his head and gave Slim a reproachful look. Slim looked to the floor and began to wag a boot back and forth.

"You a hundred percent on this idea?" Sam asked him.

"Yeah," Slim muttered.

"Well, it don't seem like a move you'd make."

Tommy worked his lean jaw back and forth and then jabbed a finger at Sam. "You know what your problem is, Mister Sam?"

Sam's own jaw jutted at this conceit.

Those at the tables stopped, ears cocked.

Tommy drew himself erect. "You just can't see past the game, that's what."

Normally, Slim would've jerked a knot on the boy's head for sassing an elder like that. But he stood quietly by, randomly wiping at a bit of infuscate drool at one corner of his mouth.

Sam tried not to return the boy's haughty look. "I see you grabbing at money, son. That what you call seeing past the game?"

Tommy averted his look. "Nothing wrong with money," he said softly.

Sam put the glass and towel down. He stepped into the boy, grabbed his jacket by the lapels, and lifted him to his toes. "Sonny boy, you got a whole lot to learn. Money ain't the name of this game. It just greases the wheels, that's all."

Slim's washed-out eyes narrowed and an angry spark rose in them. "Let 'em go, Sam."

Sam did, reluctantly.

Tommy smoothed his lapels and sniffed his ruffled dignity back into place. "You don't know ever'thing they is to know, Mister Sam."

Slim put a hand on the boy's bony shoulder. "How about you trotting on down to the grocery store and fetching us some smokes. Me and Sam need to have a word or two."

Tommy ground his teeth for a moment, and then he stalked from the place. Sam and Slim listened until they heard the pick-up engine crank and gravel crunch beneath its tires. Sam led the old man to the bar. He turned up the shot glass he'd retrieved and reached for another.

"If you don't mind," said Slim, "I believe I'll take a tall glass of water."

Sam pulled a plastic cup from the stack beside the beer tap, and he ran the cup full. Slim drank the water down without stopping and uttered an unctuous sigh.

Sam studied him. "Never seen you turn down a shot."

"Ain't like the old days," said Slim.

"Not for me, neither," said Sam. "Age, I guess."

Hardly anyone in Striven knew it, but the two were related, Sam's home here, Slim from Mobile. The two were cousins several times removed on Sam's mother's side. For a while, they caught up on family doings, and then talked of pool's nocturnal world. Finally, their capacity for triteness spent, they fell silent. Sam drew himself a beer and began to sip.

Slim cleared his throat. "Guess you was surprised to hear about me and Tommy partnering up."

"Halfway, I guess. I knowed he was follering you, and I knowed that you knowed he was a good shooter who could only get better."

"There it is," said Slim.

Sam looked the old hustler up and down again, searching for subterfuge. "You never was one for easy living, though. You always liked being hungry, being a lone wolf." Sam searched for words to match his thoughts. "A scrapper, that's what you always been. You always loved scrapping for your dough."

Slim had slid onto one of Sam's barstools, his boots on the seat's lower brace. He looked down and began to waggle the foot again. Finally, he eyed Sam and gave him a weak smile. "Always did want a son." He daubed a knuckle at a hint of ooze on his lower lip. "Doing it this way, though, it saved me from ruining him 'fore he could grow up proper. Wouldn't have wanted that on my conscience."

The gaunt old man began fingering the lip of his shirt pocket. Something was missing there, something that had always been a part of him.

"You ain't smoking nowadays?" asked Sam.

"Give that up, too."

Sam chewed on that for a second. "I heard you had the TB."

Slim's eyes flicked up, then back to the bar's sheen. "That's what Doc Quincey tole me back two year or so. I knowed sumpin was wrong, what with coughing up blood, and all."

"So why'd you send Tommy after smokes?"

A parched-lip grin found its way onto Slim's haggard face. "It's a joke between me and him. When we hooked up, he was full of hisself, trying to be a man, lighting one smoke off another. Anyways, when I finally tole him about the TB, he quit, too. Now, smokes is really Life Savers and Tootsie Pops."

They chuckled together.

The pool hall door opened to Tommy, who carried a paper bag. They were having snow flurries that day, and he knocked a bit of the melting white from his jacket. He spoke to Donnie for a minute, laughed, and then turned toward the bar. As he walked, his demeanor changed. The swagger of a teen on a good roll settled into an adult's purposeful stride, albeit one that seemed slowed by some deeply rooted onus. He gave Slim a shoulder pat, reached into the bag and lifted out a handful of candy. Slim stuffed the pieces into a jacket pocket.

"You got a glass of water for Pops here?" Tommy asked. He unscrewed a pharmacy vial and handed Slim a capsule.

Sam smiled at the moniker. Tommy had been without a father since his third year, his mama hard put to support the two of them. She'd taken in sewing and wash, had worked off and on cleaning Doc Quincey's office. When Tommy turned twelve, she started taking jobs as a baby sitter. Pretty soon, he began showing up at Sam's, and the late-night shooters more or less took him on as a mascot. His mama found out in no time, but with the menfolk at Sam's so protective of him, she sighed and looked the other way. Then the boy started staying later, learning the game and its physics. As boys will do, he sometimes overreached, as he'd done when he'd challenged Slim that first time, right there in that old pool hall. By Sam's reckoning, most young folks were rash to a fault, and that was the rest of the reason why his temper had foreshortened when Tommy rattled on so about contracts and money. But Slim, even in his newly undemonstrative way, seemed able to reel Tommy in when he got too cocky.

Sam again ran Slim's cup full of water. The careworn old shooter palmed the medication into his mouth and washed it down.

"He's gonna need another cupful," said Tommy. "That medicine keeps him thirsty."

Slim drank the next cupful's remainder down in one gulp. Sam poured another, and the old man drank that one down.

"You okay, Pops?" asked Tommy.

Slim nodded.

"Then I'm gonna see if I can skin Donnie out of a few bucks." He returned to Donnie's table, pulled out a wadded twenty, fingered the creases flat, and slapped it onto the felt. He went through a wall rack holding Sam's house sticks until he found one that satisfied him. He and Donnie lagged for break.

Now it was Slim's turn to study Sam. "You upset at Tommy?"

"A little bit."

They watched the boy examine the table and call his first shot. A striped ball clicked into a corner pocket, the cue ball back-pedaling neatly to its original position.

"You need to cut him some slack," said Slim.

"Don't like the way he's been using you," said Sam.

"It ain't what it seems," said Slim. "They's a bigger picture going on here."

"Maybe. And maybe you don't see he's riding your coattails to what he thinks'll be fame and fortune. When he gets where he's going, he'll drop you cold."

"Ain't that."

A long pause, both men oblivious to bystanders hooting at a long, two-bank shot Donnie had just made.

"The TB's got me by the short hairs, Sam. Tommy, he's using our contract as c'llateral. I'm going to try out a sanitarium in Montgomery, see what they can do for me. That's where we'll be tomorrow, after we visit with his mama."

Slim's pronouncement fell on Sam's ears with the impact of lightning that had struck too close to home. He peered down the row of tables. Just a glance at the boy, full of swagger and guile, and Sam could've taken him for Slim three decades earlier. Funny how you never know people, though, until you see how they are with the folks they've gotten close to.

CHAPTER IX

For a while, none of them spoke, each seeming lost in a scattering of memories from that ancient time – the war, the craziness that had bled the country white because of it. Sam was telling the truth, but gently. Returning soldiers were spat on, taunted, their wartime traumas and injuries ignored by almost everyone, and that included the military that had put them on the firing line. It was as if the whole damned country was trying its best to forget the war had ever happened. The nebulous cloud of collective guilt born from that Asian adventure seemed to color everything about life in the U.S. back then, probably as deeply debilitating as the guilt burdening German and Japanese citizens in the years following World War II.

At home once again, but locked into their separate hells, ex-soldiers drank, smoked, and injected themselves into altered states in order to maintain the isolation they desperately needed to come to grips with a life of peace. Still, they held their heads high when they could manage it – as if the war's outcome hadn't mattered to them, anyway, as if the ones with draft deferments and their consequent good jobs and contented families didn't count for much, as if the nightmares, the night sweats, the moods, were a part of everyone's life, as if daily survival were the only right thing to these ex-soldiers' lives.

Ironically, some of those returning wanted another war – a chance to do it right, as they came to explain it. And some wanted even more: the next war, and the next, and the next – because sometimes fighting your way out of a corner is all you feel you have left.

Sam, though he'd tried not to think about the war, and could hardly have put words to it anyway, hadn't managed to evade such self-imposed estrangement. On his return home, he needed those long months of sleepless nights, the solitude, the simpleminded back-and-forth of that broom in his uncle's pool hall. The only friends he could rationalize in that quietly deranged state were the ones who had left Nam in body bags, and the ones who had gone to the four winds following their return to The World. No, those months in the bush were the miraculous birth of Sam's adult soul, but they were also the baggage of that birth.

Thus, isolation within a world that seemed deaf, dumb and blind where basic human compassion was concerned appeared to be the only way that promised him – and his fellow soldiers – escape from those war-born birth pains. And so, even after all these years, coming home – a real homecoming – remained for Sam a dream just over the horizon.

A TALLADEGA WEEKEND

Sam and his friends had argued for days over whether to take the lesser road to Talladega for race day or the long way around on the Interstate. The trip had been Sam's idea, and he'd urged a leisurely drive through Birmingham, with a stop for lunch at a rib shack he knew of off the bypass there.

Why you wanna do that? Donnie had groused. *We can eat ribs right here in town anytime we want to. We'll have to be off at the crack of dawn if we go that way. 'Sides, I want to get to the track and set my camper up. If we get there early enough, I can go talk to some of the drivers Saturday afternoon,* he added. Donnie had won a forty-dollar pit pass from a Montgomery businessman in a game of nine-ball, the pass good for a visit to the pits, where crews would be fine-tuning their racecars, and maybe, just maybe, a few famous drivers would be hanging out there.

Archie wanted to get to the racetrack no later than early afternoon to enjoy the meet-and-greet as spectators arrived, so he voted for the more direct, rural route, through Sylacauga. Wilson had agreed, adding a pitiful postscript that girlfriend Noxanne's van was on its last legs and might not make a trip through Birmingham.

On Wednesday, as the tiff grew in volume, Sam slapped at his bar's surface with a hand towel. He hadn't expected to be ganged up on, especially since he'd sprung for the cost of seats for these four, as well as for himself and a date. But he'd finally given in, and Donnie, Archie, Wilson, and Noxanne had turned as happy and expectant as so many kids on Christmas Eve.

They began to assemble at nine a.m. in the parking lot at Sam's Place. Sam's pick-up sat loaded with foodstuff, bags of ice, four cases of beer, a washtub for icing the drinks, a half-dozen folding chairs, an overnight bag, and a pair of sleeping bags. Donnie rumbled up in his Dodge Ram pick-up and pulled in behind Sam. He carried a gigantic homemade barbecue grill lashed to the truck's bed with a spiderweb of bungees. His pop-up camper trailed behind. Then Wilson nudged Noxanne's clattering van forward until it touched Donnie's camper.

Archie brought up the rear in his eighty-four Olds. He'd hoped to ride with Sam, but Sam had insisted on Friday that Archie take his car or ride with one of the others. *Why?* asked Archie. *Luann*, said Sam (or Lu as he most often called her now), *she's gonna ride with me*.

Sam now glanced to Lu as she got out of her jeep and climbed into his truck, and then he leaned out and slapped his door panel. "Okay," he yelled, "next stop, Waffle House."

They ate for a while in near-silence. Lu was a new addition to the crowd, and no one knew yet what to make of her. Finally, Noxanne swallowed her last piece of pancake, sucked at a bit of bacon caught in her teeth, and eyed Lu.

"Y'all been dating, I guess."

Lu scooted a hair closer to Sam, who was deep into a blush. She patted his hand. "Sam's been good enough to take my mind off retiring from the Army these past months. Good to have a friend at times like that."

The ice broken, conversation turned briefly to race day, and then they struck out for Talladega. With the other vehicles strung out behind, Sam glanced right, smiled, and sighed his content. The sun still hung in the east, and its light enveloped Lu like an orb of luminous praise.

Noticing his blissful look, she asked, "What, Sam?"

"Just looking forward to race day, I guess. You sure you don't mind spending all weekend at NASCAR?"

"No, of course not. I like the intensity." She winked. "It keeps me feeling young."

He was glad she liked stock car racing; it was good to have things in common with the woman you were attracted to. He'd been driving down to Fort Rucker to see her every other Sunday or so since she and her brood of female medics had stumbled onto his place the previous summer. On his first trip down and nervous over their age difference, he'd shown up with his pants halfway unzipped and his new white shirt mis-buttoned. He even tripped getting out of his pick-up at the Dothan spaghetti emporium where they ate dinner. Their conversation alternated long spates of silence with awkward prattle, and as he drove her back onto the Army base, he was sure she wouldn't want to see him again. Instead, as he opened her door to walk her to her quarters, she pulled him in and kissed him. *Wh-what'd you do that for?* he said. *Because I like you, Sam*, she replied.

The second and third dates went better, much better. On that third night, she suggested in her soft-spoken way that they rent a motel room, and there they prepared to make love for the first time. Sam fumbled his pants off, unsure at his age that he could make enough of a go at sex with the thirty-something Lu. Then he caught her eying him while baring her prosthetic leg.

It turned out she wasn't remotely self-conscious about the prosthesis, though. She joked about it, and it even took on a name and a role in their foreplay. He came twice that night, something he'd not done since his brothel-diving days during his tour of duty in Vietnam. In fact, that night in the Dothan motel had left him with a spring in his step and feeling thirty years younger. He'd told her so over the phone the next night, and maybe that was why she'd just made the remark about the intensity of NASCAR races keeping her young.

"You know I'm causing quite a stir with your friends," she said.

"You don't pay them no mind," he said, "'specially Noxanne."

She laughed softly and rubbed his shoulder. "If I can handle training girls right out of nursing school for war duty, I can handle Noxanne."

"People tend to underestimate her."

More quiet laughter. "Now, don't go telling me she's complicated."

He smiled. "Well, she is, a little."

A line a half-mile long snaked down the road to the raceway, and it took an hour for Sam's caravan to edge up and gain direction to the blue infield camping area. Archie strode off to meet their neighbors. Donnie set up his camper, and then he fired the grill while Sam sliced up a pair of chicken carcasses. A German shepherd began sniffing around Sam's tailgate kitchen. He tossed necks, gizzards, and livers to the dog, which she pawed and nibbled, and then chomped with gusto. When she was done, she looked to Sam with a greasy grin and wandered off.

Donnie grilled the chicken cuts to a golden hue. Noxanne brought out her special potato salad, full of celery and green onions. Lu chipped in a loaf of bread and some fiesta beans, and with Sam's beer, they had a fine supper.

Soon, the sun stepped up its drift toward the western horizon. A breeze wove through the vehicles, mixing a montage of aromas. Donnie made a chicken sandwich and took off for the pit road. Wilson and Archie began a two-handed game of hearts in the bed of Donnie's truck with a half-dozen new friends looking on. As if from a choir of tone-deaf angels, CD and radio music rose above the infield. Just beyond Sam's group, a pair of bikers tried unsuccessfully to spray beer on a lithe blonde dancing atop a pick-up cab.

"Think I'm gonna walk a little," said Sam. He rose from his chair.

"Sounds good," said Lu. "Which way?"

"Let's head off toward the grandstands and see if we can find our seats."

She took his hand and they made their way toward the track.

Then hoarse mouth breathing and pounding feet. "Hey!" Noxanne called out. A large tumbler of ginger ale and Seagram's sloshed as she ran. "Y'all mind if I tag along?"

Sam felt Lu's hand tighten. Noxanne had changed to her usual attire: too-short cutoffs and a skimpy tee, which screamed BIG MAMA in large red letters above a stenciled picture of her baby, Flo.

"Sure," said a smiling Lu, "c'mon."

They reached the track and crossed, Noxanne jabbering away – mostly to Sam. He'd always taken Noxanne with a double dose of salt, but this day her increasingly coarse asides over his seeing Lu were rubbing him the wrong way. Lu must have sensed his unease, because she gave his hand a comforting squeeze.

He led them into the bleachers and to their assigned seats – at mid-track on the first row, just behind the protective fencing.

Noxanne looked admiringly to Sam. "Who'd you have to rob to get them seats?"

"A beer distributor, wasn't it?" said Lu. "A fellow you've been doing business with for years?"

Actually, it was a woman, Connie, who delivered his beer and who had also helped deliver little Flo, right there on the floor of Sam's Place. He'd been grateful for the help that day, and in return he'd paid off her gambling debts a time or two. In return, she just couldn't do enough for Sam. She sent football tickets, set after set of beer glasses etched with CRIMSON TIDE and WAR EAGLES, all of which Sam gave away. Every month or two, Sam would return to his trailer to find a Styrofoam container full of filet mignons. He gave these away, too. Connie tried to make a gift of the NASCAR tickets, but Sam had said *no, I'll pay.*

"Let's see what's going on outside," he said, and headed toward the stadium entrance.

There, a guard was trying to chase away a scruffy man sitting cross-legged on a blanket outside the enclosing fence. A few crude leather craft pieces lay on the blanket before the unkempt fellow.

"I got a pass," the man said, eying the guard. "And I got this letter." He scrabbled through a camo jacket pocket and extracted a clumsily folded piece of paper.

"I don't know about this," the guard said after reading it. "Nobody told me."

Military campaign patches had been loosely stitched to the sleeves of the scruffy man's jacket. A triple bar of ribbons hung lopsidedly on his jacket's right side. Below that, a silver star. "Well," he said, "you see the Senator's signature, dontcha?"

"How do I know you didn't make this up so you can panhandle?" said the guard.

"The senator, he's an old high school buddy. He said I could sit here and sell stuff." The man shook the letter.

Lu stepped closer to peer at his ribbons. She set a fingertip on a multicolored one and tapped it.

The man's chin wattle spread as he glanced down. "That's for Panama. It's a rare one." He pocketed the letter and extended a limp hand. "My name's Mel. Mel Walcott."

Lu took his hand in both of hers. "You're trembling, Mel."

Mel eyed her. "You look like you know my ribbons. You military?"

She nodded. "You want to talk about your situation?"

He shook no, but she kept talking softly, encouraging him. Finally, his eyes flicked left and right. "Took a team of mercs back after my hitch," he whispered. "Did a little damage to the El Salvador death squads. The Senator was one of my team members. I took a bullet in the lumbar while I was there, and then some local doc gave me way too much morphine." He pulled away, straightened his footless left leg and began to rub it.

"And the foot?"

"Gangrene. Snake bite."

The guard stepped between Lu and Mel. "Sir, you're gonna have to move. We can't be responsible if something happens to you."

The man gave the guard a dark look. "You mean something worse than what's already happened to me?"

"Honey," Lu said to Sam, "you mind if I stay with him tonight?"

"Say what?" said Noxanne.

Lu looked to the guard. "He'll be all right, sir. I'm an Army medic, at least for a few more days. I'll stay with him."

"Hoo-wee," said Noxanne, "you calling Sam honey? That means y'all really are doing the down and dirty." She swayed as she gulped her remainder. "You had your head in his short and curlies already, too, I bet."

"It ain't seemly to talk like that," Sam said.

The guard went to one knee next to Mel. "You need a wheelchair? I can keep you in the first aid station for a few hours, but I can't even do that tomorrow."

"What's she got under the hood, Sam?" Noxanne chortled. "What's she use that stump of hers for, to –"

"Now you stop this, you hear?" said Sam. He took a step toward Noxanne. "If you wasn't a woman, I'd knock some respect into you."

"Sam!" Lu put a hand on his shoulder. "I can handle this." She turned to Noxanne.

Noxanne took a step back.

Lu looked her up and down. "I know you're a friend of Sam's, but I'm not fond of women who act like tramps."

Noxanne raised a fist, shook it. "Don't you be calling me no whore! Some people tried, but then they got whupped."

Instead, Lu poked an index finger at Noxanne's tee and the picture of her baby. "That's a cute little girl. Do you act this way around her?"

The guard rose and shouldered his way between the two women. "Now look, I don't want any hen scratching going on."

Noxanne pushed him aside. Then her chin began to quiver. The fist went slack and dropped. "I miss my baby!" she bawled.

"Where is little Flo?" Sam asked.

"My mama," Noxanne blubbered. "She said the races wasn't no fit place for a baby. I left little Flo with my mama."

Lu took Noxanne's hand. "Having a baby has a way of changing things, doesn't it?"

The chastened mother lowered her head.

Mel's eyes had batted wide open at Lu and Noxanne's confrontation. Now he began to quake and drool.

"I didn't mean nothing by what I said," Noxanne replied. "I was just trying to rib ol' Sam."

Lu eyed her for a moment and then said, "Here's a thought to live by, Noxanne. Don't do anything, I mean anything, you wouldn't want Flo to do."

Noxanne backed another step away and bawled again. When it was over this time, she threw her arms about Lu.

"Now, now," said Lu. "I guess being a mother makes you feel things you never felt before."

"Uh huh," Noxanne said with a sniff. "But you gonna marry Sam and make him move away. You gonna take him away from us. That's what we all been thinking."

Lu set her hands on Noxanne's shoulders. "Honey, we're both grownups. Sam doesn't want to leave his place, and that's just fine with me."

Sam bent to Mel and asked, "You got any pills for that spell?"

Mel fumbled in a jacket pocket and held up a capsule. Sam helped him to his feet and to a nearby water dispenser. Then he eased Mel back onto his blanket.

"All right," said Lu, "give Sam a big hug and apologize."

Sam shook his head. "Go get my sleeping bag," he said to Noxanne. "Lu's too. We're gonna stay with Mel tonight."

"You can't do that," said the guard.

"I-I got that letter," said Mel.

"It'll be okay," Lu said. "He promises not to raise a fuss. Right, Mel?"

Mel nodded.

Noxanne sniffled and said, "I forget the way back."

"You got to be the one to go," said Sam, "so you get on back, you hear?"

"It's okay," Lu said. "I can see to Mel while you take Noxanne back."

After they crossed the track, Noxanne ran ahead, found Wilson, and buried her face in his shoulder. Loud sobs broke up her chatter as she told him about Mel, and then about Lu and Sam being a for-sure item. The balding, rotund man hugged her close and whispered. Then he pulled a cell phone from a back pocket, pressed a number, and handed the phone to Noxanne.

She started sobbing into the phone.

Donnie trotted up, eying Noxanne. "What's got into her? She ain't never acted like that before."

"Missing baby Flo, I expect," said Sam. He didn't mention the flare-up between Lu and Noxanne. For a couple of years, he'd been growing a bit disgusted with his ragtag customers and their raucous behavior, but Lu's magnanimity just now with both Noxanne and Mel warmed him like a day of sunshine, and he couldn't find it in himself to be judgmental. Anyway, being smitten was like that, he supposed – it made you a bit more charitable where other folks were concerned. He dug his wallet from a rear pocket and handed Donnie four of the bleacher tickets. Archie, who had just walked up, reached over Donnie's shoulder and cupped a bony hand, as if trying to prevent some misbehaving breeze from stealing those precious passes.

Donnie stuck them in a shirt pocket. "You wouldn't guess in a million years who I saw in the pits a while ago, Sam. Darrell Waltrip! And then I shook hands with Bill Elliott. Did you know he still holds the track speed record here?"

"You put them tickets in your wallet, now, you hear?" Sam said. "They'll get snatched if you leave 'em sticking out that way."

Donnie did.

Sam found his and Lu's sleeping bags and rolled them together into a limp cylinder. He added an old Army

140

blanket of Lu's for Mel. These and a small cooler with some snacks and water, and he lumbered off.

"Sam!" Donnie called out. "Hey, Sam! We're having a whole bucket load of fun."

"Yeah," Archie added with a thumbs-up. "Much obliged, buddy."

Noxanne jabbed a finger in Sam's direction and turned a rapid-fire string of words to Wilson. He sighed and nodded. Noxanne trotted up to Sam. "I'm gonna help out with that Mel guy. You and Lu ought to have a little time to yourselves tonight."

"You sure?"

"Me and Wilson just talked about it, after I talked to baby Flo. I tole him I was gonna do it."

Sam gave her a one-armed shoulder hug and turned toward the track. Noxanne trailed behind with the cooler. For a single second, Sam stopped, his brow pinched as he remembered Lu's remarking to Noxanne that motherhood changes things, that having a baby makes you feel things you've never felt before. Then he walked on.

CHAPTER X

Finally, Donnie cleared his throat. "Maybe we ought not to hang out here all day. How 'bout we drive up to Lake Martin?"

Archie harrumphed. "Colder'n a well digger's ass out there."

"Breezy, too," said Wilson. He shivered.

"We ain't gotta get out in no dang boat," said Donnie. "I know a catfish place up there on the western finger we can go to."

"I know that place," Archie said. "They don't serve beer on Sunday, though."

"Don't know as I mind that," said Wilson. He belched quietly though stubby fingers. "I feel like I'm gonna toss my cookies, and another half dozen beers might just help that along."

"It was all that fried okra you ate last night," said Noxanne. "And that big ol' breakfast this morning didn't help none." She was about to turn and offer a consoling hug when he stepped back to expel another pungent belch.

Archie peered to the bar. "You going, too, Sam?"

He glanced their way and sniffed. "Nah."

Noxanne strode halfway to the bar and punched stubby fists into her hips. "Yes you are, too, Sam Witherspoon."

"Yeah," Wilson and Archie said in unison.

"Okay, then," said Donnie, "it's been decided. We'll swing by and pick up Lu if you want to."

Sam grunted, and for a long moment he didn't move. Then he sighed, rose, and pulled on his jacket.

"Hot dog!" said Archie. "Good for you, Sam, get you out of that rut."

THE ROAD

Sam closed his newspaper and peered across the bar at the man in the worn-thin white shirt and two fingers-wide navy blue tie. Everything about him seemed slapdash, the sort of manner that urged others to deal cautiously with him, lest they be caught up in some carelessness or other. "Beer or whiskey?" Sam asked.

"On duty, I'm afraid," said the man. He looked to the wall behind Sam, then to the rafters above. A resolute smile crept over his sallow face. "Are you the owner?"

Sam gave him a wary squint. "Sam Witherspoon. You ain't from the State Patrol, are you?"

"No, no," the man said, extending a hand. "I'm Nathan Funderburk, from the Department of Transportation."

Sam nodded slowly as he shook the man's hand. "Well, I can tell you about the road out yonder, if that's what you're here for. The local kids rip-snort down it at more'n eighty mile an hour. And I need more gravel on the shoulder so my customers don't get stuck. I ain't one of those gimme types, now. Just a few loads of gravel, and get the State Patrol out here to slow the kids down. I don't want my customers having to risk their skins when they get out on the road."

"I don't think you'll have to worry about that with what I'm prepared to say, Mr. Witherspoon. Is there somewhere we can talk in private?"

As Sam looked to the nearest pool tables, he noticed Donnie's and Archie's ears perking up. They were his best customers, but also the nosiest. "We can step out back, I guess."

He returned a half-hour later without Funderburk. Scowling, he grabbed a bar rag and began a violent polishing of the oak bar's deep finish. One wide swipe upended a stack of plastic beer cups and sent them clattering to the plank floor. Four shot glasses followed. He grabbed a broom, circled the bar, and began pushing the glass shards into a pile. He snatched up the plastic cups and flung them against the rear wall. He swore, loudly. Then he straightened, growled his throat clear, and turned toward the tables.

He hadn't noticed the silence. No cue balls clicking. No boasts or laughter. Just a few, rasps as his customers' shoes sanded the dusty floor.

Archie, the shooter Sam most trusted to babysit the pool hall in his absence, rolled his cue onto the table and sidled toward the bar. Sam could be dark and moody, and in the throes of such temperament he could be home to a storm.

"Sumpin wrong?" Archie asked.

Sam's eyes narrowed to slits. "Hell, yeah." He palmed his way around the bar, snatched up the phone, and jabbed in a number.

145

Five minutes later, the pool hall's front door opened to Lu, Sam's live-in for the past six months. She crossed the silent pool hall and hugged Sam.

"Some fellow from Montgomery was just here," he quietly informed her. "The Highway Department's gonna build that bypass around Striven after all. It'll connect in right about here. They decided to widen on this side, and they gonna four-lane with a big grassy median. Gonna plant flowers in it. All of which means they plan on buying me out."

Lu pulled up a barstool, sat, and began to rub her leg stump, just above the prosthesis Army doctors had put in place. "Buy you out? What does that mean, Sam? They're going to relocate you?"

He shook his head and frowned at the gaggle of shooters edging into a broad semicircle before the bar. He waved them away. "Y'all get back to playing, you hear?" he shouted.

Feet shuffled, but no one moved. Sam's jaw firmed.

"Sam," said Lu, "they're your friends. Tell them, too."

Sam's shoulders hinged forward as he looked from face to face. He knew every one of them, their families. He'd seen most of them married, had thrown birthday parties for their children. Lu was right; they were the closest thing to a family he'd ever had. He told them in a halting voice what Funderburk had said. That Judge Collins, who owned the four hundred acres on the road's opposite side, had exerted influence. That the judge had wanted the road widened to Sam's side so he could develop his property into a trailer park and a small strip mall. That the State of Alabama would take Sam's property by condemnation if he didn't agree to Funderburk's terms, which meant payment according to something called the highest and best use of his acre and a half.

"You gonna set up shop somewhere else?" asked Archie.

"The vote last fall went against zoning, 'member?" Sam replied, voice rising. "If we was zoned commercial here, I'd get double. As it is, I won't get enough to relocate."

"When they gonna buy you out?" asked Archie.

"It won't be until after next summer. They's money problems right now, so I got a little time to figure out what to do."

"Let's go home," said Lu. "I think we need to talk."

Sam cleared out the cash register, tossed the door key to Archie, who would keep the pool hall open until midnight. Then Sam and Lu drove home.

Lu began a load of clothes and fed Luther, their blue tick hound. Sam headed outside. He replaced a few warped boards on the front deck. As the sun faded, he went inside, pulled a beer from the refrigerator and switched on the TV. Minutes later, Lu opened another beer. She muted the TV and sat on the coffee table, blocking Sam's view of his favorite game show.

"We have to talk about this, you know."

Sam picked at his beer bottle's label with a forefinger. "Ain't used to it, Lu. I ain't used to making decisions with somebody else."

"I know."

He looked up to gauge her mood and noted only a concerned expression. He gave her a tentative smile. "I didn't mean that to sound like I don't want to."

She wriggled an inch or so closer and bent toward him. "And I don't want to coax you into doing something you don't want to. I just thought we should think it through, and talking might help, that's all."

Sam sighed. Another sheepish smile. "How'd a nice-looking gal from Ohio end up with a broke down old pool hall keeper like me?"

Lu smiled and put a palm to his face. "I don't remember you being so broken down first thing this morning."

He couldn't help but refresh his smile at the mention of their post-dawn coupling. Then, as if caught in some childish prank, he sobered and straightened. "You know what I mean. The only jobs around here is over at the paper mill. If I was to take a job there, I'd get all the dog work. Besides, they don't like the way I part my hair over there. Never did."

Sam had worked at the paper mill as a young man, before he'd been sent to Vietnam, only to return and find his position filled by an old friend, Travis Wilhite. Travis had made off with Sam's girlfriend, Lora, too. So Sam had flattened him right there in front of the mill's main office. That had ended any chance he'd had to work for the mill, so he'd taken the only other work he could get – sweeping out his Uncle Cliff's pool hall, the pool hall Sam now owned.

"Surely they've forgotten about that," Lu said. "What was it, thirty years ago?"

"'Bout. But that ain't it, anyway. Some of their swing shift workers come over to my place after work. I make 'em behave best I can, but after they spend eight hours smelling mill fumes, I don't have the heart to keep 'em from a few beers and shots. Some of 'em get a little sideways, and then they end up in jail. The paper mill manager don't like that. He'll be raising a smile to the sky when he finds out I lost my bidness."

Lu sat back, took a swig from her beer. "Okay, Sam, I don't want you beating a dead horse. Forget the paper mill. We're not that far from Auburn. You could use the condemnation money to relocate over there."

"Property's 'spensive over that way, so I'd have to borrow money. And 'sides, it wouldn't take but a couple months for them college boys to tear the place up."

"Okay," she said with a sigh, "I'm fresh out of ideas."

Sam leaned back. Luther hopped onto the couch and curled up next to Sam. Finally, he said, "I got a few thousand saved up. I guess I could build over on the Montgomery Road if I could find some cheap property. I'd still be in the county, and my regulars could still come."

"But you implied to Archie that you couldn't afford it."

"Archie don't need to know my goings-on. He's a fine fellow, but he's a gossip. If he found out I had a nest egg, it'd be all over the pool hall. Ever'body'd be asking for loans."

"You really think you can pull this off, Sam? If you want to do this and don't have enough, I can chip in."

"I got enough. I can pull it off."

Lu slapped Sam's leg, her expression somewhere between humor and exasperation. "You've already decided, haven't you? Sam Witherspoon, you aggravate me to no end."

He eyed her to make sure she was kidding, and then he returned her smile. "I tole you, I don't know much about making decisions with somebody else."

Days and weeks compounded, and Sam could find no site for a relocated pool hall. Some lots he looked at were remote or too expensive. Others were ideal, but the owners weren't willing to sell off portions of their parcels. I only want two acres, Sam would say, maybe just one and a half. Road frontage, of course. Sorry, Sam, the owners would reply, I can't do that. I might cut you off a parcel along the property line, though, back in the woods. No, I need the drive-bys, Sam would counter. And besides, I can't afford to build that long a driveway.

Then one day he hurried home to find Lu soaking the soreness out of her leg stump in a tub of hot water. "Hey, sugar," he called from outside the bathroom door, "I think I might have something on a lot."

He heard splashing, followed by a dull thump. He frowned. "You didn't hurt yourself, did you?"

"I slipped, that's all," said Lu. "No harm done. Can you help me up?"

He threw the door open, grabbed a towel, and gently hoisted her up and out of the tub. He helped her settle onto a stool he'd made for her, and he began rubbing her dry.

Laughing, she took the towel. "I'm not helpless, Sam. I've just lost some of my leg strength since I left the Army, that's all."

She re-attached the prosthesis. Then she put on the bathrobe he held out and followed him to the living room couch. They sat with Lu's prosthetic leg angled across Sam's lap.

"Okay," she said, "now tell me about the lot."

Deep in thrall to her unblemished, cherubic face, he drew a blank. Since her Army discharge, her brown hair had grown to a longish length, and that added to her beauty. He scooted closer and ran his stubby fingers through it.

She took the hand in both of hers. "The lot, Sam," she said, smiling. "There really is a lot, isn't there?"

He settled back against the couch's armrest. "You know Widow Armstrong? No, I don't reckon you do. Anyway, she lives to the west of town, over on the Montgomery Road, and she's decided to sell some of her land. Leastwise, her kids talked her into it. She's had to get some long-term care – some women to sit with her and cook and clean up. Selling off some of her land's the only way she can afford it."

"It's suitable, right on the road?"

He nodded. "And guess what? I wouldn't even have to build a place. The part she wants to sell has this big barn on it. All I'd have to do is floor it, put in some heat and lights and air and dump some gravel out front. Then I can hang up my sign."

"You sure she'll go through with it, Sam? Sometimes people get cold feet when it comes to selling off their property."

"She wants us to come to her place right now and go over the details. Then she'll take it to her kids."

Lu dressed and Sam drove them across Striven to the woman's house. A dimming arc of October sunlight crowned a stand of loblolly pines to the west of her farm. Sam shut off his pickup's engine.

"Y'all come on in," a throaty female voice called out before Sam could rap on her screened door.

They found their way across the shadowy living room. Sam bent and gave her a kiss on the cheek and then stepped aside to introduce Lu.

The old woman eyed Lu for a moment. Then a grin lit the age-scrawled face. "I heard Sam got him a Army girl, and a young 'un to boot. But nobody tole me you was cute as a button. Come here, honey, and give me a hug."

Lu did.

"Y'all eat yet?" Mrs. Armstrong asked.

"No, ma'am," said Sam.

With Sam assisting, the old woman rose from her rocker. She led them to the kitchen. "I got some fried chicken left over, and some potato salad," she said. "Y'all sit down and let me make a couple of plates."

Lu helped her, and as they ate, Sam told Mrs. Armstrong what he had in mind for the barn and lot, and the price he could afford.

The old woman sipped a cup of black coffee and listened. When Sam had wound down, she said, "I hear you let a lot of devilment go on at your place, Sam."

"Well, no, ma'am," he said. "Just a few times I –"

She waved a hand. "I don't guess I mind a little whoopee, but my kids will. I tell you the truth, they ain't gonna be happy about this. I don't mind selling to you, but I got to find a way to keep peace in the family."

Sam understood. Already word had gotten back to him that church folk on this side of town were starting to grumble. This has always been a God-fearing place to live, they were saying, and a pool hall ain't nothing but the Devil's workshop. He thought for a moment of the two brothers who had killed one another in a knife fight in his parking lot, and he said, "I swore if I got me a new place I'd keep it on the right side of the law. I always tried, but I guess things got out of hand a time or two. I won't let it happen again."

She rose, pulled a quart Mason jar from a shelf, opened it, and poured until her remaining coffee turned the clear brown of lake water in autumn. She held the jar to Sam.

153

He knew from the gesture that as far as Mrs. Armstrong was concerned this consummated their deal. He sipped from the jar and handed it to Lu.

"You talk to that little sawed-off chief of police," the widow said. "Tell him what you got in mind. Then you tell him to come talk to me if he's got any complaints."

Sam and Lu complimented the liquor and food and stood to leave. Mrs. Armstrong insisted they stay long enough to eat two broad wedges of homemade peach pie. Then she took in their hugs and hobbled behind them to the front door.

On the way home, Sam began to chuckle. Lu touched him on the arm, just above the elbow. This was a phrase in the non-verbal language already growing between them, her way of asking what underlay Sam's humor.

"You ain't had the misfortune of meeting Wayman Tucker yet," said Sam.

"The chief of police?"

He nodded. "He's crooked as a dog's hind leg. Has his hand in gambling, dope, bootlegging, and half a dozen other such things hereabouts. Judge Collins, the fellow who owns the land the other side of the road from my place? Well, Tucker heard about the original road alignment, from somebody in Montgomery. He went to see the judge and tole him all about it. That's when the judge used his influence to move the road over on me."

"I knew it was probably like that around here," said Lu. "I heard that sort of thing happened around Fort

Rucker when I was there, but I guess I just wanted to stick my head in the sand and not think about it."

"Best way to be, I guess," said Sam. "Won't get in trouble that way."

"But you weren't laughing about that."

A smile. "Mrs. Armstrong may be getting up in years, but she knows things. I expect she's got dirt on ever'body in town." The smile grew to a chuckle. "Maybe even a little bit on me. Won't nobody give us any grief as long as she's around."

"It'd be easy to underestimate her," Lu admitted.

Sam began thinking about the move. It would be strange – there had been drinking and pool hall gambling in his place for well over half a century, and his regulars would be upset about the move. They'd hate the new place at first, but they'd get over it. Eventually, they'd admit the move was a good one for all concerned – and so would Sam.

He glanced to Lu through the truck cab's semi-darkness and took her hand. First she'd walked into his life like the angel she was, and then this new location had fallen to him, despite the judge and the police chief and whomever else. He began to wonder what he'd done to warrant such good fortune.

CHAPTER XI

Archie, Wilson, Noxanne, Donnie, Lu, and Sam had finished their catfish platters and were alternately spearing food particles with their toothpicks and contentedly tsking air between their teeth. As they'd eaten, Sam's spirits had slowly, almost imperceptibly brightened. He told a couple of bawdy jokes and even reflected happily on his boyhood life in Striven. Now a waitress filled their tea glasses.

"Them's fresh fish awright," Archie said to her.

The waitress smiled and nodded toward the waters beyond the restaurant, where the sun was catching every ripple, creating a thousand bright winkings. "They slept in the lake last night."

"What's in them hushpuppies?" asked Noxanne. "They about the best I ever tasted."

"We put a can of beer in each batch of batter," said the waitress. "That's what you noticed."

"I'd of never knowed it," said Wilson. "No buzz or nothing."

"Cooking boils off the alcohol," said the waitress, "leaves nothing but that good, rich taste."

Sam nodded, smiling. "I'll have to try that on my next fish fry."

The waitress left, and Sam and his friends quieted.

"You used to throw fish fries all the time," Donnie said, *"back when you had voting booths in your place. Maybe you ought to go back to that."*

Sam's smile turned sober. "I ain't into such high mindedness anymore. You know what the city fathers did after they agreed to put voting machines in there. Tried to boycott my place as a voting location. Don't know why they bothered putting them in there in the first place."

"They didn't want us who lived nearby voting," said Archie.

"Yeah," Sam muttered.

The waitress brought the check, and Sam reached for it.

Wilson snatched it away. "Ain't gonna happen," he said.

"That's right," said Noxanne. *"We all gonna chip in and buy yours and Lu's for a change."*

Sam said nothing, his face tinged with blush. He shrugged.

"There it is," said Archie.

Donnie nodded solemnly. "About time we started setting some things to rights, Sam."

THE ALBINO CATFISH

Archie clambered up the steps to Sam's Place, slapped at the hasp on the door – the lock was gone. He issued an unquiet oath and peeked in. The pool hall was a hollow, silent shell at nine in the morning, Lu the only one there. She was gathering plastic cups, shot glasses, napkins, and a few other bits of flotsam left atop the bar from the previous night. She looked up and smiled at the gangly man.

"Hot dog!" he said. "For a minute there I thought I left the door unlocked last night."

Lu smiled. "You did."

Archie swallowed. "No kidding?"

"I'm kidding," said Lu. "But you did leave a mess in here."

He let out a slow whew. "I beat feet outta here soon's I could last night. They was a football game on." He strode the length of the shotgun-style building, picking up newspapers, wadded napkins, and swizzle sticks as he went.

He'd sat in for Lu in Sam's absence the night before and had had a few too many beers on the house. He'd sloshed more than he'd drunk, and now as he stepped through the glassy islands of dried beer behind the bar, the soles of his new hunting boots gave off a series of soft pops. He looked about for the mop. Lu pointed. It leaned drunk-like in a restroom corner. He wet it in the lavatory and began swabbing his beer spills.

"Sam took the Interstate up to Georgia, I reckon," he said as he swung the mop left and right.

"That was the plan," said Lu. The mention of Sam's impromptu hunting trip with a childhood friend caused her brow a fleeting wrinkle; for some reason she had a bad feeling about it. But Sam was probably just using the friend's out-of-the-blue phone call and offer to hunt as a diversion from worry over a road widening and, hopefully, a relocation of the pool hall. She opened the fridge and began sorting the jumble of sandwiches on the top shelf.

"Who was that ol' boy he was going hunting with?"

"Frank Callaway, I think he said. Some fellow he knew here when he was a boy. You know him, I think."

Archie stopped, grasped the mop's handle at the top with both hands, propped on it as if it were a walking stick. "They was some Callahans lived hereabouts when we was boys. But I was a little bit older'n them kids."

Lu straightened. "Callahan. Maybe that was it."

Archie nodded. "They was strange folk, even for the Irish kind. Ol' man Callahan was a doctor, as I remember it. He had a place over towards Auburn, worked all hours. Had a boy and a girl. That bunch was all over the town for a while after they moved here, but then all of a sudden they wasn't a one to be seen."

"That *is* a little strange," said Lu. She made grocery

notes on a small pad of paper and shut the fridge.

"Yep. Somebody was passing rumors that someone or the other in that house was sick. From the way the family stayed holed up, they must of stayed sick a long while." He shook his head. "Then they up and moved."

"Well," said Lu, "Sam said he'd only stay in the woods a couple of hours. He'll be back tonight."

"Huh. That's a little quaint in itself. Most times you couldn't run Sam out of the woods with a stick when he's hunting."

Lu frowned, deeply this time. Sam had been nothing other than forthright since they'd been a couple, but he hadn't said anything previously about this Frank person. She cleaned the change out of the cash register, counted out twenty dollars' worth, returned it to the register, and began fingering the rest into paper coin wrappers. Well, she thought, he'll make up for that moody silence of his tonight. He always comes back from the outdoors in good spirits and wanting to tell me all about it.

I was gonna meet ol' Frank at a spot near Lake Jackson, which is 'bout in the middle of Georgia. Hell of a note. I had to get up at four in the morning in order to meet up and then pick my way down that winding dirt road in the early morning light. I was some fifteen minutes late getting to the meet-up point, and Frank was pacing around like his life depended on me getting there right on the dot. He run over, put a big bear hug on me, said how much he'd been missing me all those years, then handed me a egg sandwich and poured up a couple paper cups of coffee from a thermos. He chattered away for a while like he had ants in his pants, but pretty soon he calmed down and we went to hunting.

Now, Frank ain't never been the easiest person to be with in the woods, so while we looked for squirrels that morning, I took to keeping some distance between us. The trail rose up to a bluff over the mouth of the Yellow River, where it widens and then turns into Lake Jackson. We walked pretty close to the edge, and you could see the river's meander working its way back upstream into a patch of fog. The sun was just beginning to climb past the trees. Light glimmered and frolicked in maybe a thousand places along the other bank downstream. A large willow put a fat triangle of shade across the river beside me, and the water was so clear you could see straight and true to the bottom.

"There's a reason for it," said Frank. He edged up to the bluff's rim and hung his toes over it. "There's a reason why the water's so clear."

"Uh huh," I said.

So he talked on 'bout the mud from last week's rains, how the water had cleared up, and how the oaks along the banks weren't dropping enough leaves yet to turn the water brown.

Lu had just finished sweeping out the pool hall and had returned to the bar when the front door banged open. Lucious Everhart, the parcel deliveryman, sidled in sideways with a stack of boxes so cumbersome he could

161

hardly keep them balanced atop one another.

Archie ran to help. He laughed as he took the top three boxes. "They ain't as heavy as you was making out, Luce."

"I believe we got glass on the inside," said Lucious. "Need to handle 'em careful-like."

Lu frowned. "Bring those over here. Let's see what this is all about."

Archie and Lucious set the boxes on the bar. Lu arranged them in a neat row, drew a penknife from her pocket, and slit the tape on the first box. Out came a cascade of Styrofoam peanuts. Inside she found smaller cardboard boxes with more peanuts stuffed between them. She pulled out one of the smaller boxes, opened it, and held a shiny crystal beer glass up to the light. On one side **Sam's Place** had been professionally etched.

"Awright!" said Archie. "That'll class up the joint some."

Lu sighed and turned to Lucious. "Give me the invoice. Let me see what kind of bill Sam's run up now."

Lucious unsnapped an electronic device from his belt, jabbed at it a few times with a small plastic pointer. "They ain't no bill to it," he said. "It's all bought and paid for." He held the device so Lu could see the screen and pointed to a faint horizontal line near the bottom. "The sender asked for a delivery receipt. Sign right there, please ma'am."

Lu sighed again and signed. "What's that below the signature line?"

Lucious scrolled down. "A message for Mister

Sam. From the sender."

Lu read it aloud:

I know you've been giving away everything I send you. You just don't know how to let a person show gratitude, Sam Witherspoon. So this time I've sent you something you'll find harder to give away. Thanks again for your help, your support, and your friendship.

Connie

"Hey, I know ol' Connie," said Archie. "That's that manly gal that delivers Sam's beer once in a while."

"I know who it is," said Lu, a bit curtly.

Lucious squinted and scratched at his nappy salt and pepper hair. "I met her a time or two," he said. "She is kind of a odd duck, all right."

I fingered my Remington 12-gauge pump's safety to the on position and leaned the gun against a sweet gum. Even now that sort of morning makes me want a cigarette. I fluffed my camo jacket against the chill that still lay 'bout, and my fingers went to the shirt pocket underneath. Hadn't been a pack of cigarettes there for fifteen years, so I just took in the lake's muddy stink, alongside that sweet smell that comes to turning leaves.

Frank pulled a cigar from one of the elastic loops on his ammo vest. He held his smoke to the light, then shaved one end with his pocketknife, and he lit it. I was bending over to pick up my shotgun and was just 'bout to move away from the cigar smell and a whole spate of memories that come with it when I felt his hand on my shoulder. He pointed to a little pool beside a dead tree laying on the riverbank. It was hard to make out at first – maybe a swollen twist of paper or some plastic container that had warped in the sunlight. Then its almost-white tail flicked. It wriggled out of the shadows, and we could see the thread-like whiskers.

"Albino," said Frank.

The catfish's tail flicked again. Its two foot-long body shot upstream with a graceful kind of move, reached the deeper water, and then disappeared in an eddy.

I follered Frank down the bluff into the bottomland that fanned out to the west from the river's mouth. We crept as quiet as could be through a new coat of fallen leaves. We looked through the oaks and hickories and sycamores for squirrel nests and eyeballed the ground for telltale shreds of acorns and other nuts. We heard a whole lot of chatter and saw a good many nests, but we never had a clear shot.

The sun wasn't far from its high point when we stopped to eat sandwiches from our back pouches. Frank finished his and started inspecting what was left of his cigar. He relit it. He exhaled a long stream of smoke toward me and fashioned a smirk at the face I made.

"Can't stand being around it anymore, huh?"

I'd just squatted and leaned against the knobby trunk of a sassafras tree upwind from him, and now I started to fidget. "Wish you wouldn't do that. I'm weak on days like this."

He laughed and turned the burnt end toward his

chest and watched the red ember wink inside its white ash. "So this Lu of yours got you trained. It's what women do, Sam. They work hard to break men like us of our bad habits."

"I reckon that's so."

He inhaled again and the cigar's white ash glowed red. He whistled a stream of smoke toward me. "She must be quite a gal."

"That's the way I see it."

"I doubt she's a handful, though. You know, the way Kay is."

Wasn't much of a answer for that one, so I looked away. I was starting to wonder why Frank had called out of the blue like that after all these years. Needing a hunting partner might have been some of it, but I had a feeling that wasn't the main part. And I had to ask myself, *Sam, what made you jump at the offer? You don't usually head off to the woods to meet someone you ain't seen in ages.*

Frank started telling stories 'bout his sis, the ones their daddy used to tell when I was waiting for her to come downstairs for a date. Back then the stories got to be boring in a hurry, but I guess they was his way of sizing me up. So I used to make myself pay attention and put some clever comments in the right places. But Frank was going on and on, and before long, my attention started to drift. A high wind pushed some clumps of those fluffy clouds to the southeast, the kind you always see in early fall. Frank finally got done with his stories and balanced his cigar on the trunk of a rotting oak. He slipped away to piss. When he got back, he looked to the spot in the skies that I had taken to.

"All right, Sammy boy, tell me about it."

"Tell you 'bout what?"

He folded his arms over that big belly of his. "About you and Kay."

"What the hell you talking 'bout, Frank?"

He eyed me for a minute. "About what's going on with you and Kay, that's what I'm talking about."

Well, we'd just been talking 'bout me and Lu. What's he think's going on between me and his sister? I'd always wondered if Frank was a little off the beam, so I decided the smart move was to play along, see what was what in that fevered mind of his. "Nothing to tell," I said.

"That's not what she says."

His drooping face didn't give me any idea as to where this was heading. "She still talking 'bout me?"

He spat. "She wouldn't talk to her big brother about you. She told Cindy a few things, that's all."

"And now you're snooping, that it?"

"No, no, Sammy boy." Then he thowed a sad glance my way. "You and Kay are all I have left, except for Cindy." He pulled another cigar from his vest and tossed it to me.

I picked it up and peeled off the cellophane wrapper, sniffed it a coupla times, and stuck it in my shirt pocket.

"Go on," he said. He tossed me his lighter. "I won't tell."

At first, the smoke burned my eyes, but then its taste started to pick me up. We smoked for a while.

Squirrel chatter came to us from somewhere across the bottom. A pair of hawks circled overhead there.

"Look," said Frank, "Cindy said a couple of things. If you need to get something off your chest, I'd rather it be with me than in the heat of the moment with Kay."

"All right. Maybe I should."

"Then tell me what's on your mind."

I sat astride the sassafras' gnarly roots and leaned hard against its spine. "It's not the same between us anymore, you know that."

"Not the same." His smoke had died away again, so I tossed him his lighter. He relit it, then studied the ash that formed.

"She wasn't dependable. I don't know, Frank, she's your sister. Maybe I shouldn't be talking 'bout her like this."

He sniffed and followed the hawks. "We'll keep it man to man."

"All right, then, when I think 'bout Kay I think control. Ever'thing had to be her way. Take smoking, for instance."

He grunted.

"She badgered me night and day until I stopped the first time. That was bad enough, but then I found out she'd gone back to it herself."

He frowned. "She doesn't smoke, Sam. Take my word for it."

"I kept seeing cigarette butts in her car, with lipstick on 'em." That was fact. I figured, even at that tender age, that smoking wasn't a healthful thing, and at the time I kind of liked Kay, so I wanted her to quit. If she did, I might of quit, too.

"You've been going through her things?" He squinted and exhaled, and the smoke snaked its way across the ground toward me.

"I smelled it on her, Frank. She didn't just smoke a little bit. She smelled like she'd been rolling around in it. It was all over her clothes." I didn't tell him 'bout the way she used to sneak around to drink back then. Oh, we all used to do that, so our parents wouldn't know, but she'd tell us she wasn't, and then she'd show up late for some meet-up or other, staggering and smelling like she'd been using Jack Daniel's as perfume. I'd drop her off early at home, pissed as she could be and spoiling for a knockdown, drag-out fight. She'd yell a little bit and I'd tell her to shut up, and if she didn't, I'd get her daddy out there to sober her up. So she'd crank that old Chevy of hers and peel off for points unknown. Then just before dawn, she'd show up scratching at my window screen. I'd let her in, man smell all over her, and she'd be crying and saying she was so, so sorry for the way she'd been acting.

"Even if she does smoke," said Frank, "it's not enough of a thing to get upset about, is it? Christ almighty, you're making it sound like she chopped somebody into little pieces."

"It never was the smoking. The main thing? It was just plain dishonest, 'specially after all the grief she used to give me 'bout it."

He grunted and didn't reply to that.

I took a last puff, stubbed out the cigar on a

sassafras root, and tossed it. It bounced off the dead oak and landed at Frank's feet.

He picked it up, sniffed it, and pitched it in the bushes. "Let me give you an idea of what she's been telling Cindy."

My tongue was on fire. I pulled a water bottle from my pouch and sipped until the burning eased up.

"She said you two hardly speak anymore. That you keep to yourself. She asks you what's wrong, and you won't even talk to her. She cries about it all the time."

I knew I couldn't tell him 'bout the fits I used to see her have. It'd start all hunky dory between us, and then she'd get wild-eyed. She'd scream at me and start thowing whatever was at hand. Accusing me of God knows what. All of which is why I broke up with her. She took that real hard, too. But even then I had to wonder: was I the only one to set her off like that? She never took it out on anybody in her own family?

"Is that what she tole you?" I said. "Well, she used to cry, Frank. She cried a lot. And none of it was ever my fault."

He jumped to his feet, found my cigar, and mashed it and his own stub into the dirt with a boot heel. "She works hard, Sam. She works all the damn time. She has to let off a little steam." He stepped toward me, and something deep and hard was shining in his eyes. "She's a lot like me, you know." Then he laughed, but you could tell he'd forced it. "I guess it runs in the family."

"That's just making excuses, Frank. You know damn well she has a problem. Always has."

"You're talking about my sister. My flesh and blood. I don't like you going on about this. I don't like it one damn bit."

I pushed back until the sassafras bent. "I thought we was gonna talk 'bout it man to man."

He took another step toward me. I got up, and we stood nose to nose. We was like that for a little bit, and then his eyes softened some. He put a hand on my shoulder.

"We're family, Sam. We can work this out, I know we can. You don't have to divorce her."

"You kidding me? Is that what she tole Cindy?"

"Yeah, Sammy boy, that's what she said. She said you want to leave her. She told Cindy she doesn't want a divorce. She wants to make it right. She wants the two of you to see a marriage counselor."

I backed off a step, then another. "Now, don't take this too personal, but whatever part I played in our splitting up is none of your damn affair."

Lu looked to Archie, then to Lucious. "You through with your route already?"

"Pretty close," he said.

"Want a quick game of hearts?" Archie asked.

Lu gave Archie the house deck and pushed a couple of the boxes down the bar to make room. He shuffled and she cut. She looked to the clock. Almost noon. Maybe Sam would be home before long.

I turned and picked up my gun and walked on

back to the bluff over the river. Another catfish was floating along where the albino had been. This one quivered, black against the brown river sand. It waved its head to and fro and shot toward the deeper water. It joined three others there. Something else kind of shone in the water, and I took it at first for a piece of junk, but then I realized it was the albino. Something 'bout the fish sure was attracting me. It was there in the open, kind of naked-like. How could a fish like that ever survive? I wondered. Then the four swam on upstream.

"They's a lot of odd ducks 'roundabouts," said Archie.

"What?" Lucious asked. He threw the king of diamonds and picked up the hand.

"I was still thinking about ol' Connie. Takes all kinds, I guess."

Lucious laughed to himself and then glanced to Lu. "Nope. Just got all kinds."

They laughed and Lu sluffed a black ace. "Lucious," she said, "you get around more than anyone. You know the people of Striven better than most."

He and Archie both eyed her. "I s'pose so," Lucious said. "What you getting at?"

She looked away and tapped one of the cardboard boxes. "Oh, nothing, I guess. I was just wondering how the folks in town see this place."

"Sam's Place? Well, shoot, this place is always a topic of conversation. But I s'pose you figured that much."

"Sam runs a honest place," said Archie, clearly miffed at the conversation's direction. "Ain't nobody got call to criticize."

Lucious chuckled. "Well, Mister Archie, I don't believe that's what Miz Lu's getting at."

"Right," said Lu. "I'm just curious about how the townsfolk see us. Do they think we're, you know, from Mars, or something?"

Lucious scratched his chin for a moment. "Well, no ma'am, that ain't it. I s'pose they all work hard as can be at farming, or they work theyselves to the bone in that stinking ol' paper mill every day. They don't understand how folks can just sit around shooting pool day in and day out."

"It's a dang game!" said Archie. "Ever'body needs to play a game or two now and again."

"Yes, sir, but they don't shoot pool at church, you know what I mean?"

"Then they think we're wicked," said Lu.

"Not even that," said Lucious. He paused. "I guess all that can be said about it is they don't try to understand people they don't see and talk to ever day."

A shot rang out from somewhere in the bottom. Another, then two more. I ran fast as I could through the underbrush. Frank stood in the middle of a little grove of black walnut trees, and he was firing through the branches. He fired three more times after I got there. Then he reloaded and fired again. The squirrel nest had been set into the tree's main fork, almost hidden in what was left of the foliage. A resident chattered, mad as could be, in the quiet between the shootings. Frank fired again. The nest's wattle shook. One side came apart. Then the whole thing came loose, and the chatterer leaped away. The nest bounced from branch to branch, coming apart a little at a time. Ten feet or so above us, a half-dozen pink shapes bounced against the tree's trunk and then fell to the ground at our feet.

Frank picked up one of the hairless bodies and inspected it. "They're not supposed to mate this time of year. It's not right. It's unnatural." Then he swatted the infant squirrel with his gun's stock, and it disappeared into the brush.

The one I picked up was still alive, its eyes closed, with its mouth opening and closing without so much as a peep. "You ain't s'posed to fire through nests," I said, "don't you know that? It's unsportsmanlike." I pushed the tiny fellow at him on my palm. He swung the gunstock.

It took a minute to get the throbs in my hand under control. "Damn it, Frank, you just don't know where to draw the line, do you?"

"Where do you think I should draw the line, Sam?" he said. "Can you tell me that?" He was panting, and his eyes widened a little bit, full of excitement, it seemed, and just a hint of sorrow.

I rubbed the hand hard against one leg. "You need to calm down, Frank. You need to think 'bout what's going on here."

"Go to hell, Sam." He ejected the spent shell. Another clicked into the chamber.

I fingered my safety, let the gun slide to a ready position, and I backed off.

He stepped forward. "What're you running from, Sam? Come on. I wouldn't hurt a fly."

I took a quick look at the fork where the nest had been and backed another step.

"Come on, Sam. Stop it. Stop the running."

"You're sick, Frank. You got medicine for times like this? I bet you got some of it with you."

"I said stop it. Don't say another word."

"Or what, Frank? You gonna shoot me full of holes like you did that squirrel nest?"

His shoulders slumped a little. "You're family, Sam. I've always thought about you that way. But you can't talk like that, not about Kay."

"I ain't family. I'm sorry, but that's the way it is."

"Come on, Sam. We're not so bad. You'll see. I looked you up because we had some good times back then, and so did you and Kay. If you go away, Cindy won't let me come out here again. We have to stay together, Sam, we have to. If we can stay together, everything'll work out."

Now I was starting to get it. The whole Callahan clan had this deep, dark secret. They was all off the beam. Wild as a bunch of bugs on a hot stove. They'd made a family thing of it, I reckon. I know a little bit 'bout such, coming back from the Nam like I did with my head 'bout to explode. I took lots of phone calls that first year back, buddies of mine, guys I humped the boonies with. And some of 'em never did make it all the way back. The worst part of it was, I just then realized why Frank had got me out in the woods – it was all 'bout what was going on at home between him and his wife, Cindy.

"We aren't like them?" said Lu. "How do they figure? We're working people. We pay taxes. We go to the grocery store and the doctor, just like them. We just have a different sort of job, that's all."

Archie raked in a hand. The game over, he stacked the cards, shuffled, and dealt again. "I know what Lucious is talking 'bout."

"Okay," said Lu as she arranged her hand. "What?"

"Well, I bet after that time you spent in the Army you don't see things the same way as folks hereabouts. The ones that ain't never been in the service, much less in a war."

"Got that right," said Lu.

"That's it," said Lucious.

Lu played a low heart.

"You need to quit hitting her, Frank," I said. "You shouldn't of ever hit her. Not even the first time."

He let his shotgun's butt slip to the ground. Ever'thing 'bout him slumped until he was sitting cross-legged, face in his hands, the gun across his lap. "I know it, Sam. I know it." He spoke through his fingers, his head moving back and forth. "I haven't been good to her, have I? Cindy's such a great girl."

"That's right. And Kay needs help, Frank. She's

sick. She inherited it. You both did."

He started to sob. "I know it, Sam. I know it."

"Okay then. You got any of that medicine of yours?"

His crying settled into sighs and coughs. "I take it sometimes, but it doesn't help much. Cindy makes me take it with me when I'm out, but I thought I'd be all right today." He sniffed and looked up through the trees. "It's so nice out here. I thought we'd have such a great time in the woods, just you and me."

"You have to take it all the time, Frank. This is what happens when you don't take them pills." I scanned him for any sign of where a pill container might be. "Where'd you put 'em?"

"I think I put them in my back pouch. Would you look for me?"

I moved to his backside and pulled the zipper open, shook a capsule from the pill container, and give it to him with a bottle of water. He drank the whole bottle. Then he slid flat on the ground and shut his eyes. I picked up his shotgun and jacked the last shell from the chamber. After a while, he sat up with his eyes bloodshot and his face puffy.

"You need to do the right thing. When you get home, let Cindy call the doctor."

"I will, Sam. I promise."

We picked up our things and walked on through the woods in the direction of the Yellow River, and then upstream. The afternoon wind started pulling leaves from the tree branches. Some landed on the water. They floated across the sun's reflection and then off toward the lake. We stopped for a little while and watched them fall, and I tried not to think 'bout what Frank almost did.

He pointed to a spot at midstream. The albino was hovering there, all alone. "She's something, isn't she, Sam? No one ever bothers the albinos. You know why? They don't fit in the way people think they should. They don't play the old game of hide-and-seek. Sometimes people look at them and marvel. Did you know some folks think they're sacred?"

"Sacred?" I wanted to throw a rock at his damn fish, but Frank had calmed down, and so I decided against upsetting him again.

"That's right. If they're unprotected like that, then it must be for a reason. There's a reason for everything, you know."

I spat into the water.

"Some people think they're freaks of nature, but they're not. Well, they are in a way. They're here to get our attention. To make us see things in a different way."

"Uh huh."

"Do you see it, Sammy boy? I wonder if you really do." He turned an odd look my way, like he could see through me.

"Sure," I said. "I think it's right special to see the albino. We might not see one like that again."

He nodded. "Did you notice how beautiful she was, there in the water, just below the leaves? You wouldn't have noticed that if she'd had color."

"No," I had to admit.

He smiled and turned away, and we tramped up the riverbank to the dirt road where we'd left our trucks. He give me his keys. I asked him what for and, ever so pitiful, he asked me to drive him. He looked like he'd pretty much come to his senses by then, so I said no, he should drive his own self back home, it'd do him good. Finally, after I agreed to tag along in my truck, he took his keys, cranked up, and drove, slow as a Saturday night drunk.

Cindy answered the door. I introduced myself, and the two of us got Frank to his recliner. She turned on the TV for him and left a call for the doctor. Then she follered me outside.

I tole her what had happened at the lake. She took it in. Then she tole me 'bout his sister. Kay was committed a long time back, a few years after I stopped seeing her. Their mama had gone loony, too. And their daddy, the doc, he shot hisself. After that, Cindy busted out in tears. Frank called out to her a minute later, so she said goodnight and went inside.

After I got out on the Interstate, I called Lu to tell her I was okay, and then I rolled down the window and let the cold air in. The hum of the cars that passed took on a musical tone, and for a while I keyed on that and didn't think 'bout nothing.

An eighteen-wheeler roared by and cut in, just off my front bumper. I whipped left, then right, and two more semis pulled even with me, one on each side. I wanted away from their noise, I wanted to speed alone down that long, open stretch of Interstate toward good ol' Alabam'.

Behind me, the lanes on both sides filled up, with the three semis leading, like we was a wave of energy rolling on toward the horizon. It felt good to be moving along with such a powerful force, so much better than being caught up in something like the set-to I'd just had with Frank.

I let my thoughts take me back to those years with Frank and Kay. Hell, we was just kids then. The world was brand new for us. We turned up ever rock, looked in ever dark corner – you know, looking for a way out of the grip life seemed like it had on us. Things change, though. Eventually ever'body finds a way to live with what life dishes out, which generally ends up meaning we all go our own way, and before you know it you get old and you look in the mirror, and you realize for the first time ever that you're all alone, no matter how tight you are with family and friends. And then you think 'bout people like Frank and Kay, and you wonder, if things had been a little bit different, you might of added their craziness to the way things was turning out.

Well, I stayed in that crowd of vehicles for a long while. But something kept pulling on me, saying go on, Sam, step on it, pull around 'em, get on back home, where you belong. Finally, I did pull away, but that was only after the sun had slid past the horizon and the thinned out homes and the billboards and signs that directed me to the west.

CHAPTER XII

The day had turned out sunny and vibrant, the sky a clear expanse, as rich a blue as the Gulf of Mexico, where it deepens south of Mobile. Donnie rode with Wilson and Noxanne, Archie with Lu and Sam. Lu, who sat between the two men, turned off the radio and motioned for Archie to crack the rider's side window. For the next twenty minutes or so, the only sounds coming to them were the pickup engine's hum, the hissing of the truck's tires against the pavement, and the shrill complaint of wind as it buffeted the gap in the cab's side window.

"Sam," said Lu, "you really ought to thank everyone for our dinner."

"I did," said Sam.

"No, you just shrugged and let them pay."

"It's awright, Lu," said Archie. "He's done a bunch for us. We don't need no thanks."

"Yes, you do," Lu replied. "It's just common courtesy."

"Aw, Lu," said Archie, "it don't matter. We're all friends."

"Okay, okay," said Sam, "I'll thank ever'body proper when we get back to my place."

"Good," said Lu.

"Hey, Sam," said Archie, "I just 'membered sumpin. You was good friends with that Irish doc's bunch when you was a kid, right?"

"For a while."

Archie tee-heed. "You was better'n friends with ol'...what was that gal's name?"

"Drop it," Sam growled.

Hardly chastened, Archie winked at Lu. "Ol' Sam, he didn't get around much back then, but when he did, boy-damn-howdy."

Lu shook her head and then elbowed Archie playfully. "Now, you know the last thing I want to hear about is Sam's past lives."

Archie frowned. "Past lives? You believe in that stuff?"

Lu laughed softly. "I mean his B.L. lives."

Archie's eyes almost crossed with bafflement.

"Before Lu," she said.

That had them laughing, even Sam.

A STRANGER VISITS

Although the ides of April had barely passed, a wave of summertime heat was baking the town of Striven. The previous day, Sam had wiped away a sea of sweat and packed for an overnight fishing trip to breezy Lake Martin. He'd wanted Lu to go, too, but she'd insisted on keeping the pool hall open. Two months earlier, Sam had turned over the ledger books to her. She now paid the bills, kept his bank accounts straight, and had already managed to settle his back taxes. Too, she'd been gently reeling in his habit of bestowing freebies on the customers. This had quickly established her reputation for parsimony among the drinkers and shooters at Sam's Place, and her husbanding of the pool hall this day was only fanning those embers.

It's April, she'd replied when her customers began grousing about the building's swelter, and besides, it's supposed to cool down tonight. One of the shooters suggested turning on the huge fan in the building's gable. Not until noon, Lu replied, nodding toward a large, galvanized cooler. We have plenty of cold water if you don't want to buy beer, and I'll tell you what, I'll open the front and back doors. We'll have a nice breeze through here, and you'll forget all about the heat outside. They didn't forget, though; a discordant hum filled the place as they drank Lu's water and lined their shots.

But Donnie seemed preoccupied with something more intimate. Striven's most accomplished pool hustler slipped from his barstool and hurried toward the restroom. He'd been impacted for a week, which had left him deeply out of sorts. He stayed in the restroom a long while. When he emerged, followed by a fetid cloud, he jumped high and clicked his heels.

"Hallelujah!" he shouted. "I broke free!"

The shooters nearest the restroom slammed their cues to the table and turned away, noses buried in the crooks of their arms. "Holy Moley," said one, "you been eating 'possum again?" His tablemate could only laugh into his elbow and move upwind.

Lu rubbed her smarting eyes, sighed, and turned on the gable fan.

Thus unburdened, Donnie looked to the tables for a game. It had been weeks since any of the regulars had been willing to take him on in a twenty-dollar round of nine ball, and he had no takers this day. So he reclaimed his stool at the bar. He looked to Lu and tapped the oak surface. "I think I'm gonna celebrate," he said.

Still rubbing her eyes, she replied, "As well you should after leaving that behind."

"Think I'll start with some beers and shots," he said, "and then we'll see what's what."

Donnie had never been a problem drunk. Some drinkers turn mean after an overflowing measure of spirits, while others sit slumped over the bar, telling morose tales to any who will listen. Donnie, though, was a happy drunk, prone to laugh at anything short of death and taxes. Any comments others might make about his upwelling silliness would likely lead him to raise foolishness' stakes even higher. And, if some humorless soul felt compelled to accost him over all this, he'd shift to his trademark pranks. So between tips of the cup, he told Lu every bawdy joke in his repertoire. In fact, he so enjoyed the telling that he began them again. Lu rolled her eyes as the juvenile sexual innuendoes and the scatological asides, and that was all it took to send Donnie's comedy to a more ludicrous plane.

Just after noon, he settled into a new pitcher of beer and chomped an overstuffed barbecue pork sandwich Lu had had in the refrigerator for a couple of weeks. Soon his stomach began to rumble. He leaned sideways and let go a resonant blast.

"Go!" Lu shouted, an arrow-straight arm and forefinger directed toward the restroom.

After another extended stay, he emerged from the toilet giggling and began to fan the door.

"You are such a child," she said. "I don't think even marriage would've made an adult of you."

"Marriage?" The giggles rose a half-octave. Then the frequenter of hookers and loose women marched around the nearest table, humming snatches of Wagner's wedding march, including a painfully off-key rendition of its trumpet fanfare (Striven's mayor, Hosea Karp, had been known to broadcast a recording of this piece onto Main Street via a loudspeaker system whenever he got wind of an upcoming wedding). After three laps, Donnie wove his way back to the bar and bought another pitcher.

"You drink this," Lu said as she set the pitcher in front of him, "and then I'm cutting you off."

He gave her a bleary-eyed sad clown look.

She smiled in spite of herself. "I mean it. Drink up, and then get on home."

A while later, he slid from his barstool and wove a sinuous path to the restroom to pee, but the room was occupied.

Just then, a squat presence darkened the front entrance.

Lu peered the length of the building, trying to discern who this was. She still didn't know everyone in Striven, but the plump man with the sweaty forehead and blank look didn't appear to be a local. This might be, she considered, a lost traveler happening on Sam's Place. More than likely, though, he was the real estate appraiser Sam had told her was coming for one more talk about the State's condemnation of his property – one phase of a planned road widening out front. She waved and said, "Help you?"

The man stepped in and looked around, as if unsure the place was safe to enter. A seersucker suit clung loosely to his pear-shaped frame, evincing minor weight loss. He shrugged off the suit coat, pulled a handkerchief from a rear pocket, wiped his balding head and rosy cheeks, and stared at the still-waving Lu. "Are you the proprietor?"

"Yes and no," she said. "You're from Montgomery, aren't you, about the road project."

Two of Sam's regulars, Noxanne and Wilson, had followed the man in. "Texas, according to his car tag," said Wilson.

The man turned, gave the couple an exasperated look, and waddled toward the bar. He wore thick, wire-rimmed glasses that magnified his beady eyes. "I made a wrong turn," he said. "I stopped in town for directions, and during a passing word or two, the grocer mentioned this as a gathering place. Do you have an interest in politics here?"

Politics had grown contentious everywhere over the past couple of years. The mere mention at Sam's Place of goings-on in Montgomery and Washington could very well result in fisticuffs. Sam had warned Lu about it: So if anyone comes in and tries to rabble rouse, head it off, pronto.

Lu eyed the man. "Mostly drinking and pool shooting. Sam Witherspoon's the owner. He offered this place to the county once as a voting site, but some of the locals had concerns about coming to a pool hall-slash-bar to vote. And the city fathers apparently did everything they could to discourage voting here. So, no, we're not about politics."

Undeterred, the man extended a soft, white hand. "My name's Lark Honeycutt."

Donnie edged up behind Noxanne and Wilson. "Hey," he whispered all too loudly to Wilson, "what's up with the baby-faced guy?"

Honeycutt turned, sighted Donnie down his pug nose. "I believe I have the floor here, fella."

Lu shushed Donnie before he could issue a rejoinder. She turned to the man. "You have business here, Mr. Honeycutt?"

"He's from Texas," Noxanne said to Donnie. "We saw his car tag. Big ol' Caddy. I bet he's some big dog back there."

"Peckerwood's one a'them highfalutin city types, 'f you ask me," Donnie slurred.

Lu frowned, shook a finger, and again turned to Honeycutt. He asked her to confirm his directions back to the Interstate and then to Atlanta. Lu took him to the bar and drew a map. Then, his tone confidential but loud enough for the curious to hear, he droned on about how Lu and her fellow Alabamians should eschew government's social safety nets – and about how doing so would revitalize both person and nation.

When he'd wound down a bit, Lu said, "You're some sort of Washington type, I take it."

"You could say that." He mopped his face again. "Can you turn on the air conditioning? I'm not used to this humidity."

"Fat chance of that," said Wilson, who had sidled up. "She's tight as a tick when it comes to money."

Honeycutt smiled approvingly and said to Lu, "You must be a Republican, then."

Lu shook her head. "I was recently discharged from the Army. They didn't encourage politics."

He faced the others. "How about the rest of you? Alabama's a Republican state. Surely you must have Republican leanings."

"Not me," said Wilson, "Politics is just a barrel to put bottom feeders in." Several of the other shooters yeahed that.

Donnie had groped his way around the bar and drawn a foamy cup of beer, which he'd downed in two swigs. He drew another. He chugged that and, since Lu wasn't paying attention, he drew a third.

"I see," said Honeycutt. "Then you folks have Tea Party sympathies."

"What?" said Wilson. "What kind of tea party?"

"Don't you know nothing?" said Noxanne. She slapped Wilson on his broad behind. "They dress up in them funny clothes and three-cornered hats. Then they parade around and pretend they back in olden times."

Donnie looked to the restroom – still closed. He made his way around the bar again and stood off to one side of the group.

"They're an anti-political movement," said Honeycutt, "and I have to tell you, I sympathize with their frustration. I'm trying to help organize them, to give them a political focus. Are you folks interested in setting Washington straight? If so, I can give you names and numbers –"

Donnie chortled. "Tea party?" He glanced again to the restroom. Still in use.

"Shoot, mister," said Wilson, "we got enough trouble keeping Striven on the up and up."

"Hey," said Donnie. He began to wriggle. He knocked his knees together.

"We're barely able to collect enough revenue to keep our police force and fire department operating," said Lu. "We're having hard times."

Assent burbled from the crowd.

"Hey!" said Donnie, a bit louder.

Everyone turned.

"You say tea party?"

Honeycutt's haughty look returned. He nodded.

Donnie snickered. "Well, I'm 'bout t'have a pee party." He pulled a dollar bill from a jeans pocket. "I bet this twen'y I c'n pee farther'n an'body in the house."

Tittering laughter from the crowd.

"'Cept Noxanne, o'course. She can put a rope o'pee out there a foot past anyone." Crotch cupped in one hand, Donnie stumbled, pigeon-toed, toward Honeycutt.

The Texan threw up a hand.

"C'mon," Donnie giggled, "let's pee!"

Honeycutt backed away and looked to Lu. "Would you please keep this creature away from me?"

Donnie reeled into the space between Honeycutt and Lu and said, "Shi'fire fella, I'm real ser'ous. I got t'pee real bad." He grabbed one of the man's fleshy hands and tugged. "C'mon ou'side. Be the Striven champ'ship."

Honeycutt tried to pull his hand away but, thanks to the Texan's overlarge pinkie ring, Donnie hung onto him.

"Aww," said Donnie, taking note of Honeycutt's look of abhorrence, "he don' like t'pull his whanger out in public."

For a moment, Honeycutt's hand went limp. Donnie peered at it, turned it over. Then he eyed the Texan. "Hand this sof' 'n' white ought'a be on a hooker."

Noxanne, who always bridled at the mention of hookers, jabbed a finger in Donnie's direction. "You be careful what you say, now. Don't you make this personal, you hear me?"

Honeycutt jerked his hand free and glared at Donnie. "You, sir, are disgusting. Get out of here before I call the police."

"'Kay," said Donnie, "but I got t'pee first." He reeled toward the rear door.

"The restroom's free now," Lu said. "Use it, and don't spray the whole room."

Donnie made his way there. He urinated without closing the door and began to caterwaul loudly, butchering his favorite tune, *I've Gotta Be Me.*

Lu had become antsy over Honeycutt and his political pronouncements, and Donnie's errant behavior was animating the crowd. So she drew beers for the regulars and urged them back to their games. She offered Honeycutt a draft, too, but he didn't seem to hear. Instead, the Texan wiped the hand Donnie had clung to on a pant leg and nodded toward the restroom. "Is that man a homo?"

Noxanne snorted. "Donnie? He's had more poontang than anybody in town. 'Cept for my Wilson here. They both hung like a pair of young mules."

Wilson frowned, but then a smile slowly formed. He kissed Noxanne's cheek. "Thank you, sugar."

Donnie returned, zipping his jeans. "Hey, Texas —"

"His name's Lark," Noxanne interrupted. "You believe that fruity name?"

"Well, whadda 'bout it, Lark, you need a hooker? Maybe I c'n fix you up. I know this gal 'bout your age. She's clean, 'cept she might have a few crabs left over. She won' pickle your pecker, though. Promise."

Honeycutt turned livid. "You're vile!" he said. "Get out of my sight!"

Donnie doubled over laughing. And so did everyone else in Sam's Place, even Lu. Donnie laughed from beer's elation, of course. Wilson, who had taken his share of kidding over his bald head and round belly, reveled in his relief at the joke being turned on someone else for a change. As for Noxanne, she was impish enough to enjoy anyone being mocked. But Lu — her shrill hee-hawing simply led the others in their race to humor's ecstasy. Every cobwebbed corner of the roadhouse vibrated with laughter.

As for Lark Honeycutt, he had only two choices. He could let the laughter burn away his shame, in which case he could join in the fun and be accepted as one of Sam's regulars. Or he could let the laughter's heat drive him farther away, compounding his indignation. As fate would have it, he was of the second persuasion.

For whatever reason, Texans can be like that. Not all, mind you; many are as humble and unassuming as the tree-deprived Texas landscape. Others have their heads in the clouds, thinking only of heavenly release from the mortal coil that is Texas. But some, such as Lark, see the sun rising and setting on that state of the Lone Star. Maybe, because the state occupies so much geography, and because they tend to weather its javelinas, rattlesnakes, refinery smog, infernal heat, and howling winds with heads held high, they feel they must surely stand a cut above the nation's other benighted masses.

So it could only follow that Honeycutt would edge toward the door and freedom from these scruffy Alabamians. But as he backed toward the front of the building, he failed to notice that Donnie had circled behind and was now tiptoeing up. The crowd's laughter trickled away. All eyes widened as Donnie reached, grabbed Lark's belt and pants, just above the rear pockets, and jerked them down.

A collective gasp, followed by abject silence, as the crowd took in Lark's pink silk briefs. Then the laughter began anew, a notch higher. Fingers pointed. Some, laughing hysterically, fell to their knees and slapped the dusty floor. Others rolled onto their backs, feet and arms flailing like the legs of so many upturned turtles.

"Them's some ri' pretty und'rbritches, Lark," said Donnie.

Honeycutt pulled up his pants, cinched his belt tight to prevent an encore performance, clenched his wadded suit coat in one hand, and made a pitifully powerless swing at Donnie with the other hand. The punch slipped by a tottering Donnie, and Honeycutt's momentum carried him toward the open front door.

Had the laughter not been so loud, Honeycutt would've heard a pickup drive up and park near the front entrance. He'd have heard the truck door slam, and maybe the heavy plod of boots approaching. But he didn't. Sam's titanic frame now filled the doorway, holding high a string of bass caught hours earlier at Lake Martin. "Hey," he called out. He was about to add, "Who owns that car with the Texas plates?" when Honeycutt looked up just in time to greet Sam's largest bass.

Its slimy scales kissed the Texan's cheek. He tried to straighten but, his plump physical vehicle not yet under control, one cheek slid up the stringer of Sam's catch, scales and fins nipping his jowl. Sam's customers surged closer to take in the moment. Honeycutt reeled, spewing slime, his face agleam with fish gloss and droplets of blood. He scrabbled through a pants pocket for his handkerchief, but couldn't extract it, so he rubbed at the slime with his seersucker coat.

"I heard'a people liking fish," said Donnie, "but I ain't never seen a body kiss one 'fore."

"You haven't heard the last of this!" Lark yelled into the amplified shrieks, floor slapping, and fallen-down leg kicking. He shoved his way past Sam and stalked toward his car, rubbing with the seersucker coat at the fishy scent, the coat growing more malodorous by the second.

Sam looked to the crowd, which was still aflame with laughter, then to the parking lot, where Honeycutt, with a fat finger, jabbed at his car door's combination lock. Counterbalanced by his string of fish, Sam leaned toward the man. "Hey, mister," he called out, "I'm real sorry. Come on back in and I'll buy you a beer."

Laughter surged higher at that, swirling like a whirlwind above the crowd, rising through the cobwebbed rafters, escaping through the fan's softly swooshing blades, and chasing Honeycutt's car as it slewed its way out of Sam's parking lot and into the remainder of the April afternoon.

CHAPTER XIII

As Sam pulled into the pool hall parking lot, he noticed a paper from a yellow legal pad thumbtacked to the front door. Lu, sensing something wrong, set a hand on Sam's arm. Sam clambered from the truck, ripped the paper away without comment or reading, folded it, and stuffed it in his shirt pocket. He waved everyone in, drew beers for them, and thanked them properly for his and Lu's dinner. Only when they'd left did he draw the paper from his pocket and read it.

"What's it about?" asked Lu.

"About what I expected," he said. He handed her the note.

Sam Witherspoon,

> *Several of our finest citizens, on their way home from church today, noticed your truck at this establishment, along with vehicles of several of your regular customers.*
>
> *Let me remind you of the ordinance in this county prohibiting the sale of alcoholic beverages on Sunday. I <u>will</u> be by tomorrow morning to question you about goings on at your place on this date, and I <u>will</u> expect to see your sales ledger for the Sunday sales you made.*

195

Wayman Tucker
Chief of Police, Striven, AL

Lu set the paper on the bar. "What's going to happen, Sam? I mean, is there something he can do to us?"

"Harassment's all it is. They ain't much to make of it otherwise. I wasn't open to customers, and I didn't sell no alcohol."

Lu looked to the floor and sighed.

"Don't you worry none," he said. "This happens every once in a while. All that's going to happen is Tucker'll come by, make a few threats, and then we'll both go about our bidness."

"Oh, Sam, I hate this. I just hate it!"

He smiled, rose, and tugged her to him. "I was gonna leave you with the place tomorrow so I could go fishing. The only bad thing's gonna happen is I won't be able to wet a hook until I have my sit-down with Tucker."

TOUGH JUSTICE
PART 1

Hosea Karp, the mayor of Striven, was a short man. He had to sit on a phone book and set his feet on an upside-down Coke crate so as not to resemble a child behind the massive mahogany desk he'd talked the city council into buying him. This day his eyes bulged, something that occurred whenever he was troubled, and this wrinkled his forehead, nudging a graying crew-cut upward. The fingernails of one hand clacked out a rhythm on his desktop.

"The way I see it," said police chief Wayman Tucker, "is ol' Witherspoon has stepped on his pecker this time."

Billy Savewell, pastor of Striven's First Baptist Church, crossed one stick-thin leg over the other, as did Wesley Wilding, the pale, balding pastor of the United Methodist Church of Greater Striven. They nodded their agreement, although wincing at the chief's guttersnipe language.

"Well, I just don't see the concern," said Jimmy Harbin, chief elder of the Church of Saints and Sinners. "I've known Sam for a good while now. Although he doesn't seem to have much use for churches, he's a sober, upright citizen, and I don't see how he can be blamed for a little teasing done when he wasn't even there."

"Jesus," growled Judge Zachariah Collins. "Do you not yet understand who that Texan is?"

The previous day, a Texan named Lark Honeycutt had stormed into Karp's office, just as the mayor had hoisted his feet onto the desk for his afternoon nap. Honeycutt railed about the crowd at Sam's Place, saying he'd nearly been molested by a skinny, gap-toothed pool shooter. Donnie something, he told Karp. The disgusting lout was drunk, and from the moment I set foot in the place he acted as though he wanted his way with me. It was all Karp could do to keep from smiling as Honeycutt fleshed out his tale of having his pants pulled down, right there at the front door to Sam's Place. With Honeycutt's story told, Karp ventured a grin and a quiet chuckle. Yeah, he told the Texan, ol' Donnie's like that. He might pull the pants off Minnesota Fats himself if he'd ever set foot in Sam's pool hall.

Karp's reaction upset Honeycutt as much as having his trousers jerked to the floor, which had exposed his pair of pink silk briefs, a detail he'd left out of the story. *I know people*, the Texan had said, *important people. I can have you stepped on. I can have you squashed like a bug, you hear me?*

Well, what do you want from me? Karp asked. *Donnie's already pulled your pants down. I can't go back in time and make him stop.*

You can have him arrested for assault, not to mention lewd and lascivious behavior, Honeycutt said.

No, I can't, Karp replied. *Pulling your pants down isn't assault, and if anyone acted in a lewd manner, it was you, standing there – in Sam's doorway, for crying out loud – like you had a hooker on her knees.*

Damn you! Honeycutt yelled. *I'm on good terms with a couple of former Presidents of the United States, you understand me? I can have this little whistle-stop turned into a greasy spot.*

Karp reckoned Honeycutt might actually do him some damage, and he really, really wished he could go back in time and take back the fellatio gibe. After the Texan had bellowed that he was going to Montgomery to see the governor and stomped out, Karp's hands began to shake. He bent to his bottom drawer and pulled out a pint jar of Mrs. Armstrong's corn liquor. He took in three strong belts. His face grew rosy and his ears burned, and it thus took mere moments for Honeycutt's threats to dwindle to nagging whispers.

Still, Karp thought, he should make a gesture, something to placate this Texan. Resolving to be the town's decider, he would make a show of moving against Donnie, maybe even against Sam's Place. Old Witherspoon's pool hall had been a worrisome sore on the otherwise staid town of Striven ever since Karp had first risen to the city council, and Witherspoon's allegedly cancerous sore had thrummed particularly hard within the town since Karp was elected mayor. In fact, some of Striven's better people had recently petitioned him to stop the late night goings on at Sam's Place.

Maybe he could shut Sam's Place down for a couple of days. Donnie would be *persona non grata* around town, and besides, a couple of days off might do Sam some good. He had a girlfriend living with him now, and surely she wouldn't mind having him underfoot for a few days. First, though, Karp needed to test the political winds; he would gather the local power players together, tell them about the Honeycutt pansting, and see how they felt about it. And that had led to this morning's meeting.

"Yes, I did look into this Honeycutt guy, Judge," Karp said. "I know he's a political advisor to some fat cats in Washington, and they say he's a take-no-prisoners type. Even the folks in his own party say he can gut you before you ever know he has a knife out."

"Yep," said the judge. "Exactly right. That's the kind of fellow he is. And he can do it so you'd never know he was the one who did the gutting."

All six men shuffled their feet as they considered the image that summoned.

"I've been racking my brain for years," said Billy Savewell, "trying to figure a way to rid our town of Sam Witherspoon's den of iniquity. Now we have the opportunity to get him good."

"Amen, brother," said Wesley Wilding. He looked from face to face. "Anybody got a suggestion about how to kick this thing off?"

"Look, fellas," said Jimmy Harbin, "I really don't think you can use Donnie's pantsing to make charges against old Sam."

The chief eyed the young churchman. "You trying to tell me my business, Jim?"

"Hush, now, both of you," said Billy Savewell.

Jimmy Harbin waved away Savewell's admonishment. "Judge, you're the man who interprets the law. What do you say? Is there enough to charge Witherspoon with something?"

The judge ran a finger into his shirt pocket, which held a tiny recorder. He pressed the PLAY button. "I think it best that I stay out of this conversation for a while," he said. "The mayor invited me here to act as a judicial observer, and that's what I aim to do. And, of course, to make sure you yay-hoos don't go so far out on a limb that you can't be pulled back."

"That's right," said Karp. "I don't want anybody running roughshod over the law in my town."

The chief chortled. "Your town?"

Karp pushed himself as tall as he could in his chair, raising his toes on the Coke crate like a ballet dancer. He tapped his chest. "That's right, my town. Now here's the plan. I propose we shut Sam down for a couple of days, seal the building. Let everyone know. That ought to ease Honeycutt's pulse."

"That's mighty generous," said Chief Tucker, "given that Donnie Wimple all but molested Honeycutt, right there in the doorway to Witherspoon's place."

Karp shrunk into his chair's high back.

"We all know that won't work," said Wesley Wilding, "but if we put our heads together I know we can get Witherspoon. Give him something serous to worry about. I mean, something that'll have him begging for mercy." He winked at Savewell.

Billy Savewell winked back. "We can do better'n that if we've a mind to."

"Y'all hold on," said Karp. "You're starting to sound like a lynch mob."

"Oh, *well*," said Billy Savewell, "I think we can even do even better'n *that*."

Shoes scraped and chair legs clattered as the others pulled their chairs forward.

"What you got in mind, Brother Bill?" Wilding asked in a low voice.

"Now, just wait a damn minute," said the judge. "You aren't going to hatch a plot this morning. Word'll get out, as it always does. People know who's in this office right now, and if you do something to bring the State Bureau of Investigation or some other legal interloper in here, I'm not going to be made a party to it."

He spun a cautionary tale about a judicial colleague who'd sought to sort out a case brought by a northerner, a tourist passing through, it had seemed at the time. A fellow who had gotten lost and, after his CHANGE OIL light blinked on, decided to have his car serviced by a station in a town north of Striven.

The station proprietor and a couple of his cronies had been drinking all day. The northerner's companion, a long-legged brunette, had to use the rest room. She climbed out of the Lincoln Town Car to a chorus of howls and whistles. While the proprietor changed the oil and the northerner took his turn at the rest room, the owner's pals groped the brunette (who wasn't the man's wife, as it turned out), whereupon she scratched them deep and wide with her dagger-sharp fingernails. After the station owner made all due apologies for his cronies' behavior, the man paid for the oil change, and the couple drove off. Then, fifty miles down the road, the car's oil filter came loose. The oil drained out and the engine seized up. He had to leave the Lincoln and rent a lesser car to drive back to his residence, which happened to be the governor's mansion.

A pair of east coast reporters had unearthed evidence of the governor's liaison in New Orleans with the leggy brunette. They had traced the governor's trail south and discovered the tryst, then north to the oil change, the groping, the scratching, and the two men's ensuing hospitalization. Then they'd found the Lincoln in a dealer's repair shop in Montgomery. When the governor arrived home, a horde of reporters met him at the gate. The governor handled the flap with some agile spin, and the next day he sicced his attorney general on the Alabama town. And that had the town teetering on the edge of bankruptcy.

"Honeycutt could do that to us in spades," the judge told Karp and the others.

"There, you see?" Karp said. "You boys don't realize what you're messing with. You need the law on your side. Let that rattle around in your heads for a while before you consider doing something stupid."

Wilding gave him a condescending look. "You think you represent the people, Brother Karp, but you don't. The people listen to *us*, and when it comes down to it, *we're* the law. You're going to hear what Brother Bill has in mind, and then we expect you to handle the upshot with every ounce of the power vested in your office."

Karp stood on the Coke crate, his face cherry red. These two pastors thought that since they had divine right on their side they could second-guess everything Striven's elected officials did, something that could render any mayor livid. Karp was about to suggest they stuff their opinions when Jimmy Harbin cut in.

"You're wrong, Brother Wes. The citizens won't stand with us if we do something patently illegal."

Wesley Wilding sniffed. "I always had you pegged as a mamby pamby type, Brother Jim. Why, you don't have enough God in your soul to tie my shoelaces."

Billy Savewell added an amen and turned a smug look Wilding's way. Then he said to Harbin, "I'm afraid the secular cancer that's infected this country has poisoned you, too."

This was the sorest of points with Harbin. He'd heard about sermons from Savewell's and Wilding's pulpits, rants admonishing him for admitting drunks, druggies, harlots, and same-sex types into his church and condemning those inclusions as an embrace of Old Ned himself. In fact, Harbin had lost some of his congregation because of these pastors' nattering. He clenched his fists.

Wesley Wilding pointed to Harbin's hands. "See? God's vengeance is working in you too. You're just afraid to let it go."

Harbin was about to stand when Wilding leaped to his feet and thumped Harbin on the forehead – hard.

Wide-eyed, Jimmy Harbin fell back into his chair. "What did you do that for?"

"My daddy once had a mule named Henry," said Wilding, "and he couldn't get old Henry's attention unless he conked the creature between the eyes. But once he had his attention, the mule would become his obedient servant and they'd go to plowing. I gave you that thump so you'd wake up to God's will. So now it's time to lay on hands. Time for you to receive the Lord's marching orders."

Wilding nodded to Savewell, who rose, and together they put their hands on Harbin's head.

Harbin slapped them away, sputtering. "Why, I never imagined two preachers could come up with such lunacy!"

"We're just the Good Lord's humble servants," said Billy Savewell. "We don't shy away from His will, even though at times it might seem dark and ominous."

Harbin sputtered again, waved his arms in wild circles, and stormed out.

Wilding turned to the others with a sigh. "Brother Jim's lost to us, I'm afraid. So let's have a word of prayer for –"

"No, let's not," said the judge. "This Honeycutt fellow has put fish in our skillet, and it needs to be fried without delay."

Karp, who had been content to return to his seat and watch the preachers' carrying on, now realized the implications of the judge's colorfully cryptic statement: Wilding and Savewell had gotten wind of Honeycutt's pantsing the day before. Then, before the meeting, they'd no doubt hatched a plan to put Sam in his place. They'd only come to the meeting to cajole the others into blessing their mysterious plot.

"Go on, now," said the judge. "You two have things to *attend to*."

His emphasis wasn't lost on the pair. They rose, exited, and sauntered arm in arm down the street toward Savewell's church.

Judge Collins turned to the chief. "All right, what exactly do those two have up their sleeves?"

Silence hung like a hammer over the remaining three.

The chief's chair began to squeak. "Well, I didn't agree to it," he said. "I didn't want anything to do with it."

"With *what*?" asked the judge.

Tucker blinked. He made a show of swallowing and then wriggling as deep into his chair as its wooden slats would allow.

"Wayman," the judge said in a soothing tone, "it's all right. No one's accusing you of anything. Just tell me what those soul savers have up their sleeves."

Tucker looked to his mirror-like shoes.

"You'll be fine, Wayman. Just tell me. They're going to do something to old Witherspoon, aren't they?"

The chief nodded.

"What, then? What are those two yay-hoos planning to do?"

Finally, as if he'd stuck a finger in a light socket, the chief jerked upright. He lunged to the edge of his chair. "Those two, they had it planned so they wouldn't be involved directly."

"Well, any fool would figure that, Wayman. Come on now, what are they up to?"

The chief eyed Karp and then gave the judge a sharp, intent look. "They said you would want it done that way."

Judge Collins walked his chair an inch closer. He leaned forward. "Wanted *what* done, Wayman?"

Karp knew how oily the judge could be. And he now had a suspicion that his grilling of the chief was all theater, that both men knew far more than they were letting on, that the judge was orchestrating something, while at the same time distancing himself from it.

The judge turned to Karp. "What's that odd look for, Hosea? Are you in on this? Do you know what they're planning?"

Karp could no longer take the tension of the judge's coy game. He stood and backed behind his chair, barely able to peek over its high back. He swallowed. "I-I just don't think I like what I'm hearing, Judge."

Zachariah Collins studied him for a moment. He turned to the chief. "Tell him, Wayman. Tell us both what's going to happen."

Tucker looked to the floor. "They're gonna burn ol' Sam out," he said.

"I see," said the judge.

Karp wanted to hide, but the converse side of his nature was to voice his thoughts aloud when pushed to a state of extreme nervousness. "I-I bet I know why," he said. "Th-they figured Striven would have to pay to condemn Sam's building. They couldn't stand the idea, and be-besides, they wanted me to put city money into a st-strip mall on your land, opposite Sam's juke joint."

The judge smiled.

Karp took in a deep, relaxing breath and expelled it. "But they don't understand the law. Old Sam was going to get highest and best use for the land, paid for by the state. So there's no need to burn his place down."

"That's true," said the judge. "There are many, many things those two don't understand." He reached into his shirt pocket and thumbed off the recorder.

After receiving a wink from the judge, Tucker glanced Karp's way. "Naw," he said. "They know all the angles. They know the state'll pay."

Karp frowned. "Then they're gonna burn Sam out anyway. But you should know there are a lot of people around here who like him."

The judge nodded. His smile turned steely. "Perhaps Sam's not liked by the right people, Hosea."

Karp's eyes widened, his understanding dredging deeper. "If they burn Sam out, then the churches will have this town by the gonads. People won't have another place to turn when they need a little relief from their ups and downs."

"Are you saying you don't approve?" asked Collins.

Karp blinked, twice. The judge wasn't just condoning what the preachers were planning; he was in on it. It was his idea. Karp went bug-eyed. "Holy cow," he said. "Holy cow!"

Zachariah Collins said, "You're a good man, Hosea. Perhaps too good a person to be our mayor." He eyed Tucker. "You're with me on this, aren't you, Wayman?"

Tucker nodded.

"Talk some sense into Karp, will you? At least keep his tongue from wagging about this."

"This-this'll get out," Karp stammered. "People won't stand for it."

The judge rose. "But they will, Hosea. Striven's folks won't look as deeply into this as you, or for that matter, into any other controversy that comes their way. They look on such goings-on as out of their league, as a never-ending series of far-away contests. College football games, if you will. The folks here'll do what they always do. They'll cheer from the sidelines – for the *real* leaders of this community."

Karp was about to protest, but the judge waved a hand to silence him.

"Besides," the judge went on, there's the law, and then there's justice. Our townsfolk will be seeing Witherspoon receive a little tough justice for a change." He chuckled. "It'll make them feel, you know, secure, knowing it wasn't them being drawn and quartered."

He strode out to the sound of Wayman Tucker dragging Karp from behind his chair.

209

CHAPTER XIV

It was true: Wayman Tucker came by, with an armed deputy, as if Sam constituted a material threat to them, and maybe even to the town. But Sam had never kept weapons on the premises. He didn't have to; even at his age he could manhandle most troublemakers who came his way. And Tucker did drop a few not-so-subtle threats during their conversation. Sam smirked at them and, for the third, fourth, and fifth times, he calmly told the chief that he hadn't been selling alcoholic beverages, that a few friends had dropped by, and that they'd gone to Lake Martin for catfish.

Lu had wanted to stay for the confrontation, but Sam wouldn't hear of it. Minutes after the front door to Sam's Place closed behind Tucker, the phone rang.

"He tried to rile me a time or two," Sam told Lu, "but I didn't bite at it."

"Then everything's all right? No charges made?"

Sam chuckled. "He pointed one of them fat little fingers of his at me, said, 'Your time's coming, Witherspoon. You keep it up, and I'll see you in my jail. No, better'n that, I'll see you in the state pen.'"

Sam noted her slowly forming smile, just before her soft, tentative laughter tumbled out. "I'll bet that stubbornness of yours sent his blood pressure sky high."

"Don't doubt it." Sam said with an oversized grin. "'Fore he left, he turned — almost tripped over that deputy of his — and he

said, 'You never know where your next batch of trouble is gonna come from.'"

    Lu said nothing to that.

    Sam's grin faded to jaw-jutted sternness. "I started to tell him trouble just might jump up and bite him on the butt, too. But I didn't."

TOUGH JUSTICE
PART 2

Sam jerked awake. He felt for the TV remote on his lap and muted the baseball game he'd been watching. Then he reached across the sofa, found the source of the insistent, jangling noise, and answered.

"Sam Witherspoon, you're a pox on Striven," a deep, singsong voice said, as if the words were an incantation. "May God have mercy on your soul." A click.

Sam placed the receiver back in its cradle, reached for his half empty beer bottle, and took a deep swig. He occasionally got crank calls like this, always someone finding righteous indignation at the bottom of a bottle and seeking redemption by threatening the owner of Striven's only pool hall. He rose.

"Lu?"

No answer.

He stumbled to the rest room and urinated. He called her name again. Still no answer. Then he smiled, remembering.

Lu had stayed at the pool hall to tidy up and take inventory of the remaining food, beer, and pool hall supplies Sam kept on hand. She'd also insisted on working on the business' books before coming home. If we're going to run this pool hall together, she'd told him that afternoon, I won't have the tax people on our backs. We're going to keep the books straight. Sam had never tried to cheat on taxes, but he'd always run the place by the seat of his pants; consequently his recordkeeping was habitually random and inadequate. So, sure, if Lu wanted to keep tabs on that part of the business, she was welcome to it.

He went to the kitchen, found a bag of pork skins, stretched it open, and slid back onto the sofa. This crank call – it had been different, and it began to trouble Sam. The message seemed rehearsed, the words measured, as if the person really had meant business. He'd better call Lu, just in case something was up. His hand closed on the receiver as it rang again.

"Sam!" the familiar voice said. "You better get on over to your place. They's some people looking like they wanna burn it down!" This was Archie. Besides Lu, he was the only person Sam had ever trusted to run the pool hall in his absence.

"Whoa, whoa," said Sam. "What's this?"

"Your place! I just drove by and saw 'em light a torch!"

Sam threw on a jacket against the chilly April night and let out Luther, his hound. Then he lumbered to his pickup and took off toward the pool hall.

He arrived to flames licking up the front door and the gable above. A thin, silhouetted figure was throwing some sort of liquid on the blaze. As it hit, the flames brightened, and a dense, acrid smoke billowed. Kerosene.

A car door slammed and two figures came running

213

from the far side of the building, both thin, one much taller. Archie was the tall one. And he'd brought Donnie, one of Sam's regulars. Archie loped toward Sam as Donnie took a swipe at the fellow with the can. The man batted Donnie's arm away and tried to throw kerosene on him. Donnie dodged away, then ran back to Archie's car and pulled an axe from the back seat floorboard. He raced to the pool hall's rear.

"Lu's inside!" said a panting Archie. "I heard her yelling just now." Then he pointed to the shadowy stick figure with the fuel can. "That's that old traveling preacher. And his daughter's somewheres about."

Leviticus Withers and Dorene, his daughter. But why? What would have possessed the old reprobate to set fire to the pool hall? Sam took off toward the building's rear. He'd deal with Leviticus in a minute, but he'd left Lu with only a key to the front door. He had to get her out.

By the time Sam turned the corner at the building's rear, Donnie had chopped the back door from its hinges and was now at the front of the pool hall, Lu behind him. He swung his axe at the doorframe. Sparks flew. The hinges shuddered. Smoke flooded inward.

"C'mon!" said Sam. He and Archie scurried back to the building's front. The door fell in a spray of sparks onto the cinderblock steps. Donnie's axe head had come loose; it bounded down the door's length like a rabbit on the lam. Leviticus Withers staggered away from the fiery cascade. Donnie threw the axe handle to the ground and pushed Lu through the doorway. As soon as she hit the gravel, he jumped.

Lu, rising, saw Leviticus. She ran to him and swung a fist. He dodged and threw a counterpunch. She fell.

"Hit her, Papa!" a voice like a banshee wail cried out. "Smite her with the strength of God's angels!" A haggard female figure emerged from the shadows on the building's far side. Dorene.

Sam reached Lu, who lay flat on her back, pushing away from Leviticus Withers with her one good foot. Sam backhanded the gaunt man and sent him sprawling. He pulled Lu up.

"The baby okay?"

"I'm not hurt," she said, standing now. "I just got pushed down, that's all."

"He hit you," Sam said to her. "He socked you on the jaw."

"Hey!" said Archie.

Donnie was scuffling with Dorene, both cursing loudly.

"It was a glancing blow, Sam," said Lu. "The army taught me how to slip a punch."

"Hey!" Archie repeated, "What baby?"

"I'm pregnant," said Lu.

Mouth agape, Archie said, "Sure 'nough?"

Sam grabbed Archie by the elbow, pointed toward a faucet and a hose in a grassy island to one side of the building. Then he picked up the axe handle and stalked toward Leviticus.

The old man went wide-eyed with fright. Dorene had broken away from Donnie and now set her frail body

215

between her father and Sam. Sam sent her tumbling across the gravel. He swung the axe handle one-handed at the old man's legs. With so little meat on Withers' frame, the hit sounded like wood on wood. Leviticus fell with a grunt. Sam raised the axe handle over his head with both hands.

"Sam!" Lu cried out. "No!" She ran to him, one hand cupped against her paunch.

Archie turned a pitiful stream of water on the building's front. The frame and siding smoldered a bit and began to steam. At mid-building, tongues of fire probed deeper.

"Please," Leviticus moaned, "please, no!"

The axe handle fell with a crunch on Withers' left shoulder.

Lu grabbed Sam's arm, pulled him away from the old man. Dorene began cursing Sam. She swiped at him with ragged fingernails. Lu managed to kick her in the abdomen, and Dorene fell, writhing.

"Sam, please!" said Lu. "That old man didn't think this up. Talk to him, find out who put him up to it."

Sam sighed. He nodded and tossed the axe handle aside.

"You broke my shoulder," Leviticus wailed. "Oh, God, it hurts something awful!"

"If it wasn't for Lu," Sam growled, "I'd of killed you straight out."

"I know," said Leviticus. "Oh, God, it hurts!"

Sam went to one knee at the old man's side. A spear point of bone peeked through Leviticus' blood-soaked shirt and jacket. The sour smell of cheap bourbon rose from the old preacher's labored breathing.

"Why?" Sam asked. "I thought you and me was on good terms."

"I been on the outs," Leviticus said. For a second, he swooned. Then a spasm hit. He yelped, and consciousness returned.

"On the outs?" said Sam. "With who?"

"The Lord," Leviticus whispered. "His servants. Those preachers."

"What the hell you talking about?" asked Sam. "What preachers?"

"Brother Savewell. And Wesley —"

"Billy Savewell? Wesley Wilding? They put you up to this?"

Leviticus nodded. "Needed money…Me and Dorene…" He groaned.

"You could've come to me for a handout. You always did before."

"You don't understand," Leviticus whispered hoarsely. "They my brothers…in the Lord."

"They ain't nothing but a couple of polecats," said Sam.

Leviticus looked away. "You s'posed to be run off."

Sam took that in. Those two preachers had been trying their best for years to ruin his business, everything from trumping up complaints the State Patrol had to look into to intimidating his customers, all with little success. All right, the pool hall tended to place Sam in the gray, no-man's-land of the law hereabouts, but whose fault was that? He'd tried everything he could think of to give his place an air of respectability – from offering it as a voting place to holding family picnics for his customers' families, none of which impressed Wilding and Savewell and the city fathers.

"Sam!" Archie yelled. "I ain't doing no good." The water hose's thin stream fell limply into the spreading flames.

"I called the fire department 'fore I left the house," said Donnie. "I ain't sure they gonna come, though."

Sam shook his head. "They ain't gonna. Not if you tole them it's my place that's burning. Archie, you might as well turn that hose off."

Dorene had helped her father up, and together they limped toward their decrepit pickup.

"Hey!" said Sam.

They hobbled faster, Dorene glancing over her shoulder at Sam.

Donnie started after them, but Sam grabbed his arm. "We don't need to worry with them," he said. "My mind's fixed on a couple of preachers."

Donnie said, "I'm gonna roust out the firemen, then, kick up a fuss at the station house if I have to." He took Archie's car keys and drove off, rear wheels spewing gravel.

"Those two preachers, " said Lu, "what do they have against you?"

"It ain't nothing personal, I s'pose," said Sam.

"They just don't get live and let live. Life's either their way or you better beat feet outta town."

Dorene got her father into the pickup, scrambled to the driver's side, and cranked up. Its quivering tailpipe belched a cloud of smoke, and they were gone.

For the next half-hour, Sam, Lu, and Archie watched the pool hall burn. A wind had gathered, and the flames leaped like ocean waves toward the rear of the building, the walls and roof joists popping and hissing with the advancing flames. Crashes, as the pool tables collapsed. A shrill whistle grew in volume. Then an explosion.

"That's my tap," said Sam. "The other beer keg'll go up in a minute."

As it did, Lu turned to Sam and threw her arms around him.

"Now, now," he said. He brushed at her hair with one hand.

A siren howled on the road from downtown. A minute later, two fire vehicles hove into view and rattled into Sam's parking lot. Firemen began unwinding hoses. They unleashed a mighty stream of water from the tank truck.

A police car slipped quietly into the parking lot. Police Chief Wayman Tucker slid from under the wheel and strode toward the three. "I just stopped old man Withers," said Tucker. "That daughter of his had that old truck weaving all over the road. She said you assaulted her daddy."

"Damn right," said Sam. "I broke his shoulder with a axe handle after he started the fire."

"Now, you look here, Witherspoon, you can't jump on folks just because –"

Sam took a step toward the shorter man. Archie moved behind the chief to prevent retreat.

"I ain't jumping no way or no how," said Sam. "We saw him with a can of kerosene. He dumped it on the front door."

"Did you see him toss a match?" asked Tucker, as yet undaunted by the two taller men. "As ever'body knows, ol' Withers can be crazy as a loon at times. He might of thought he was dumping water on a fire somebody else started."

Sam picked up the axe handle and stepped closer. The chief swallowed.

"He admitted to it," said Sam. "And he tole me who put him up to it. Savewell and Wilding."

"Hold on," said the chief, "you can't go accusing good citizens –"

Sam grabbed the chief's shirt front with his free hand and twisted it. He lifted Tucker to his toes. "You little piece of trash, I bet you was in on it, too." He lifted the stout little man higher and drew back the stick.

"Sam!" said Lu. "You've got the high ground. Don't squander it."

Sam paused. After a long minute, he let go. The chief fell to his knees.

"You're lucky as hell, Wayman," said Sam. "If Lu wasn't here, you'd done been thrashed within a inch of heaven."

Tucker began to blubber.

Archie helped the chief to his feet. As he dusted him off, a late model Cadillac slowed to a crawl on the highway just off Sam's parking lot.

Lu took Sam's arm. "Isn't that one of those preachers?"

Lu had seen Billy Savewell sitting in the shotgun seat; Wesley Wilding had the wheel. Without a word, Sam bolted for the car. The driver let off the brake, prepared to drive away, but Sam had already leaped onto the road in front of the car. He whacked a dent in the Caddy's hood and leaned toward the windshield. He sneered. "Well now," he said, "what a nice s'prise to see you two out tonight. Come to see your handiwork, I reckon."

Wilding shrunk into his seat. Savewell lowered his window. He leaned out, his Adam's apple wobbling as if with Saint Vitus' Dance. "We-we just happened along, Witherspoon. Now-now get out of our way."

Sam sneered. "I thought I recognized that voice. It was you what called in that threat to me tonight, wasn't it?"

"I-I didn't –" Savewell said.

"Ol' Withers left a little kerosene in that can of his," said Sam. "I got a good mind to pour it on this Caddy and light it, like you did my place."

"We haven't done a thing to you, old man," said Savewell. "Now-now get out of our way before we run you over."

To the two preachers Sam's sneer no doubt inflated to demonic proportions in the flickering firelight.

"No, I know it wasn't you that lit the fire. You two ain't got the guts to do your own dirty work. You had to hire it out to that pitiful ol' Leviticus. By my reckoning, that means you two abetted an arsonist, on top of being liars and cowards." Sam turned. "Archie, bring me the rest of that kerosene."

Wesley Wilding began honking the Caddy's horn. After ten beeps, the horn stuck, its blare throbbing against the night.

A flicker of amusement rose from Sam's glare. "All right, I can't burn you, leastwise not with Chief Tucker looking on." He took a step back and swung the axe handle at one headlight, then the other. He smashed the windshield. The horn's blare stopped. Sam kicked a dent in Billy Savewell's door. "Go on, now, 'fore I decide to get Tucker to write you up for driving with busted headlights." He stepped away and the Caddy screeched off, careering down the two-lane road.

"Sam!" Archie called out. "Tucker's about to get off."

The chief had just opened his car door. Archie caught him before he could climb in.

"You ca-can't hold me up, Witherspoon," said Tucker. "You can't obstruct the law."

Sam waved, and Archie let Tucker go. For a second, the chief stood shaking. Then he broke wind.

"You mess your britches, Wayman?" Sam asked, firelight shining on his wicked leer.

Archie laughed.

"That-that axe handle," said Tucker, "put it down."

"Oh, I ain't gonna hit you tonight," said Sam. "But I am gonna keep this stick, just in case you do sumpin to change my mind. Remember, I can get enough off Leviticus and those preachers to ruin the rest of your born days. Go on, now. Git!"

The chief did, his car slewing gravel left and right.

The building collapsed. With that, the firemen crept in closer and put out the last of the flames. Sam's Place, as it had been known for some thirty-odd years, was no more. Sam poked through the debris with the axe handle for a while, and then he drove Lu home.

While she bathed, Sam fed Luther, who seemed overly antsy, as if he knew what had transpired. The dog ate a couple of bites and then heaved.

The phone rang as Sam dried from the shower – Mrs. Armstrong. The elderly widow had earlier offered to sell him a barn and a couple of acres of her land for a new pool hall he was to open after a planned road widening took his old property. She'd heard about the fire and called to tell him he could rent the place until he had things set to rights. Sam dressed for bed and lay down.

Lu lay next to him, her head on his chest. "Sam, how much trouble are we in?"

"None, I expect. Nobody in that bunch is gonna dare press charges. 'Sides, Archie's a hell of a gossip. He'll let everybody know who burned me out – and why. It won't hurt their church bidness much, but it'll sure as hell keep them two off our backs."

They lay quietly for a long while. Luther walked back and forth at the foot of the bed. Then he set his front paws at their feet. Sam didn't protest, so the dog crawled up and nestled into the folded-down bedspread. Seconds later, his eyes closed.

"You asleep?" asked Lu.

"'Bout," said Sam. "I was just thinking. I sure am glad I took out insurance on the place, like you wanted me to."

She rubbed his chest with a forefinger. "I have some savings, plus my Army retirement. You've put away some money. With the insurance money, we can start over."

He said nothing for a minute. Then he sighed. "I guess they was a lot of times these past years when I enjoyed being the local bad boy, you know? Had a chip on my shoulder, always more enjoyable being on the outs with the powers that be than finding a way to get 'em on my side." Another pause.

"When we move to Widow Armstrong's, we're gonna hang out a new sign: Sam and Lu's Place. Make a family joint out of it. Maybe serve some restaurant-style food. Have maybe four pool tables for my regulars, of course, just for old times' sake."

Lu said nothing.

He turned on his side, his face almost touching hers. "And that ain't all I decided on," he said. "You and me need to get married, what with the baby coming." He paused. "I mean, if that's okay with you. If that's what you want, too."

She put a hand to his face and kissed him. Then she turned over and he snuggled into her, one chapped hand on her stomach bulge. They fell asleep that way, the sun's first wary shards edging through the blinds.

ABOUT THE AUTHOR

Bob Mustin has had a brief naval career and a longer one as a civil engineer, and has been a North Carolina Writers Network writer-in-residence at Peace College under the late Doris Betts' guiding hand. In the early '90s, he was the editor of a small literary journal, The Rural Sophisticate, based in Georgia. His work has appeared in The Rockhurst Review, Elysian Fields Quarterly, Cooweescoowee, Under The Sun, Gihon River Review, Reflections Literary Journal, and many sites in electronic form.

To Learn More about Bob Mustin, visit:

Website: www.BobMustin.com

Blog: Bobmust.wordpress.com

PUBLISHING ACKNOWLEDGMENTS

"What Might've Been" was published in an e-zine, Imitation Fruit, in their November 2011 issue.

"The Faithful City" took a third place award in the 2012 Patricia Boatner Fiction Award (Sponsored by the Tennessee Mountain Writers, Inc.)

"The Outer Masquerade" took a 2012 first place award for fiction from the Appalachian Authors Guild (the guild is a subsidiary of the Virginia Writers Club) and went on to take a second place in the 2012 VWC-wide competition for fiction.

ACKNOWLEDGMENTS

There are many I should thank for the serendipitous happenings that led to this book. First, there's Mike Aloisi, who saw one of these stories, wanted to see more, and encouraged me to keep writing until there was enough for a book. A patient man, Mike.

While I was neck deep in this project, Lyn Hawks cast her eagle-sharp eye on most of these stories and gave me her writer/reader opinion of them. Without her help, these stories wouldn't have been nearly as enjoyable. There are others, too: Cynn Chadwick and Tommy Hays, who helped me hone my writing skills at UNC-Asheville, and my dear departed friend, Doris Betts, who sped up my development as a writer by leaps and bounds.

But most of all, I owe a debt of gratitude to Becca for understanding the space and time her husband needs to follow his muses.